# La Nuit à Therouanne

### ... A short Story ...

## Peter Gatenby

Grosvenor House
Publishing Limited

All rights reserved
Copyright © Peter Gatenby, 2023
© Peter Gatenby, Dove Cottage BA5 1PD, 2023

The right of Peter Gatenby to be identified as the author of this
work has been asserted in accordance with Section 78
of the Copyright, Designs and Patents Act 1988

The book cover is copyright to bobarmstrongartist.co.uk

This book is published by
Grosvenor House Publishing Ltd
Link House
140 The Broadway, Tolworth, Surrey, KT6 7HT.
www.grosvenorhousepublishing.co.uk

This book is sold subject to the conditions that it shall not, by way of
trade or otherwise, be lent, resold, hired out or otherwise circulated
without the author's or publisher's prior consent in any form of
binding or cover other than that in which it is published and
without a similar condition including this condition being
imposed on the subsequent purchaser.

This book is a work of fiction. Any resemblance to
people or events, past or present, is purely coincidental.

A CIP record for this book
is available from the British Library

ISBN 978-1-80381-564-0

# Contents

| | | |
|---|---|---:|
| | Prologue | v |
| Chapter 1 | The Silent Lady | 1 |
| Chapter 2 | The Rescue | 11 |
| Chapter 3 | "I'm afraid there are no roses." | 15 |
| Chapter 4 | At the Pilgrim | 23 |
| Chapter 5 | The Plan | 33 |
| Chapter 6 | The Young Recruit | 41 |
| Chapter 7 | The Waiting Game | 47 |
| Chapter 8 | The Settlement | 53 |
| Chapter 9 | The Delivery | 59 |
| Chapter 10 | The Chase | 65 |
| Chapter 11 | The Changeling | 73 |
| Chapter 12 | Serendipity | 81 |
| Chapter 13 | Too much information can spoil the game | 89 |
| Chapter 14 | "Pride goeth before destruction and a haughty spirit before a fall" | 101 |
| | About the Author | 111 |

# Prologue

This story takes place firstly in northern France, then in southern England, and then back in southern France.

To give the writing a degree of credence in relation to how the various parties might speak, much of the dialogue has been written in French. Usually, the reader will find footnotes giving the English equivalent. However, this has not been done in every case, as what is said is often what may be expected, avoiding the need for constant translation. In the final chapters particularly, there is a lot of French used, because some of the parties speaking would almost certainly not have learned any English.

To give examples, when talking about the identical twins, the phrase in French *"deux petits pois dela même pod"* should be understood or guessed at by even a junior school pupil, thus no translation is given.

However, the defence witness – the bride recalling her wedding – is unlikely to have had much of an education, and thus everything she says is in French. This is deliberate, to emphasise she is just an innocent young girl from southern France; so, footnotes give the translation. However even here where the words spoken have previously been translated or are predictable, a translation is not provided.

The ports of Calais and Newhaven are chosen to engender a degree of reality to the travels to and from France. Those familiar with these harbours will find the description will not fit with what you may find there today, or even 170 years ago.

Some astute readers may question whether the prisoner would have been put on a train to at least Lyon. However, while railways in England were being built at breakneck speed in the 1840s, in France the laborious legal procedures hampered their development. So, in 1844 few lines would have existed, and the old-fashioned means of transport would have been the order of the day.

Without giving too much away before you have read the story, some may question the legal possibility of having a defence witness appearing before the prosecution's case has been completed; not to mention a witness becoming the "prosecuting counsel". But, as they say, "why let the facts get in the way of a good story?" After all, this is a work of fiction.

*Chapter 1*

# The Silent Lady

Our story starts at a small inn on the road to Calais, at Estrée-Blanche, a short distance from Therouanne. The year is 1844, an evening in March. Although a chilly night, the two gentlemen dining are not inconvenienced, as a good fire burns on the hearth. The gentlemen sit at separate tables. One is well-dressed but slightly portly. He wears a neat beard, and his face portrays a friendly jovial man. Although not handsome in the classical sense, he holds himself well, and from his hands you can tell he has some artistic bent. Perhaps he plays a musical instrument or is an artist. The other gentleman is much lighter in build, his dark eyes are always watchful, and his dress – although sombre – is immaculate.

They dine well on veal, and although it is late neither man seems anxious to retire. The portly gentleman, sensing his fellow diner is not ready for bed, asks the innkeeper, "Une autre bouteille de vin, s'il vous plait." He speaks fluent French with ease, as it's his native tongue, but he is well educated and can also converse in English. He moves over to the other gentleman's table and strikes up a conversation.

"May I poor you a glass of wine, Monsieur? The night grows chilly, and you do not seem anxious to retire. I had this *bouteille* put aside especially for me, but a good wine is not enjoyed when one drinks alone."

"I would be glad to accept your kind offer, Monsieur, and put aside my worries for the moment."

"You are in some predicament, Monsieur? Can I perhaps be of some service?"

"No, no, it is of no matter, just various small problems. Do not concern yourself. Let us talk of other things."

"Alors, Monsieur. Have you travelled far?"

"From Paris, and I must leave for Calais in the morning. I have important business to deal with as soon as I arrive in England. Why do you journey this way, sir?"

"I also am on my way to Calais, but like you I do not rest easily with the thought of tomorrow. Tell me, Monsieur, would your spirits be lifted by the attentions of a good woman?"

"You jest, sir. I am a man of honour. No woman will lighten my burden. I am not in the habit of seeking such pleasures each time I stop the night at some foreign inn!"

"My humble pardons, Monsieur, I did not mean to give the impression that you were anything but a gentleman. An honourable gentleman, Monsieur. But if I might describe a situation where a young lady, an attractive young lady, happens to be staying at the inn. Perhaps you have dinner together and she gives you the impression that she is happy with your attention to her. Would you not seize the opportunity, if it arose? Having of course previously been most careful to check that there was no case of you forcing her into a compromising position."

"Maybe. I cannot deny in my younger days there were a few times when I did make hay when the sun shone."

"Aha, you English, you have such a way with words. I tell you, Monsieur, that I found myself in such a situation about a year ago. There is a young lady, a most beautiful and attractive lady, who wears her hair long, and it is jet black. She has a most engaging smile, and her eyes… oh, her eyes, Monsieur, that can as easily enrage a man's passion as turn him to stone. She seems to be able to speak with her eyes which, like her hair, are also black. I came across this lady not far from here at Therouanne. Indeed, I had intended to be at Therouanne tonight, but I was held up by some urgent work to a bridge ahead, which makes it difficult for a carriage to pass, especially in the dark. I trust we shall be able to pass in the morning."

"I also hope our passage is not delayed. But go on with your story, sir. Who is this lady?"

"Her name is of no consequence to my story, but as I said, I first met her at Therouanne and by chance found myself seated close by her at dinner. We did not talk while we ate, like you and I tonight. But while I was sipping a brandy after my meal, I conversed with her. She did not reply, but the gesticulation of her hands and the expression of her face and eyes were sufficient indication that she was happy with my attentions to her. Shortly, however, she took her leave and retired."

"After a short while, I also left for bed, having been entranced by her and almost dreaming of what might be. When I stumbled upon her in the hallway, I was to discover that her belongings and carriage had been held up and the coachman, who was not familiar with these parts, had already given her a favour by journeying this way. However, troubles multiplied when one of the horses had collapsed and died, and the coachman had been put to extra expense and trouble in bringing his coach to Therouanne to deliver her belongings. He insisted he be paid that night, as he had to be elsewhere in the morning. She naturally protested that her resources were limited and that it was unreasonable to expect payment so late in the day."

"I was in an advantageous position in that I immediately settled the bill. I must add that I would have happily assisted any other fellow traveller in such a predicament, but in this case, it gave me a slight advantage in that she was now in my debt.

Not that I was expecting repayment in money, you understand. Indeed, I impressed upon her that it was a gift, a favour that needed no repayment. But to be honest with you, Monsieur, I did wonder – even pray – that she might just grant me that ultimate favour that only a woman can give! As she walked up the stairs, she looked at me most intently, as if she wanted to take note of every detail of my face and bearing. As I have said, Monsieur, she had these eyes that seemed to touch one's very soul. Yet, looking up to her, I seemed to detect some distant tragedy that haunted her."

"I was left in the hallway, half in a trance. What was I to do? As I mused over the way she looked at me, while I prepared myself for bed, I could not make up my mind whether she had intended speaking her wishes but had been prevented because of others about the hallway at that time."

"After some hours, I could stand it no longer and stole myself to visit her bedchamber. This was not difficult, as her room was adjacent to mine. I crept down the landing to her room, clutching a small single rose. I had noticed it on a climbing bower that grew up the side of the inn and had only to lean out of my bedroom window to pick it. The rose was not only a pretext to enter her room and engage her attention, but I felt it was also an omen, as roses were most uncommon at the time of year."

"I knocked on the door, and when I did not hear a reply, I entered slowly. She was lying in bed in a pure white nightdress; her black hair had been brushed and combed, and she was such a picture to melt any man's heart. She sat up when she saw me, and I responded by holding out the rose. This relaxed her a little, but she did not cry out or say a word. The only light in the room came from the moon, which shone through her window as the curtains had been drawn back."

"I drew nearer and handed her the rose, which she took, hesitating a little, and in the process looked up at me. As she did so, she shuddered slightly. The light from the moon was now directly upon my face, but coming across from one side, you understand. I could not therefore precisely tell whether she was looking at me or outside towards the moon itself. She took my hand and continued to look up at me, as if searching to remember something, or just trying to remember every detail of my visage. I could not comprehend this. No woman before has, I might say, taken such an interest in my countenance."

"Suddenly she reached out to a small jewellery box on a table beside her bed, and after a few moments squeezed a brooch into my hand. Then, with her hands, she indicated that she wished me to wear it in my hat! After this, she blew me a kiss and dismissed me."

"I was, how you English say, deflated and extremely puzzled. If she did not wish me to pay her any attention, why had she not dismissed me as soon as I entered the room? Or for that matter, why the apparent signals on the staircase as she retired? And as far as the brooch was concerned, this seemed to indicate that I had been awarded some prize – but not the prize I was expecting."

"When I awoke the next morning, having had little sleep due to being puzzled by these events, I found to my surprise that she had already left. I was left in a spell for some months as I brooded over the matter, but in the end, I had to find out more about her, who she was, and where she came from."

"I therefore employed a trusted servant to find out more about this woman. For some months, he had no luck, as although I had described her in such detail as to make her unmistakable, I did not know her name, or where she normally lived, or even for that matter whether she was English, or French, or perhaps Spanish."

"Some three months passed with no news, then suddenly success. My servant in his wanderings had retired to bed in a village just this side of Calais when there came from below many sounds of people arriving. By now my servant was inquisitive of anything that may be new, as I have learnt to be."

"Over the months you develop an eye to observe one's fellow man and record their every detail, then discard it if it is found to be of no importance. I have travelled up and down this road on several occasions in the hopes of finding her again. In these months, I have learnt to read the signs that others do not take account of themselves."

"You, Monsieur, are clearly a gentleman of some reputation. You have an important mission, perhaps a matter of State. I can tell this from the papers you have in that portfolio that never leaves your side. You keep looking at it as if to check upon it. Yet no other has entered the room. The most sensitive papers, I suggest, are in the inside pocket of your coat, as from time to time you touch them, apparently to check they have not fallen from your pocket. The troubles you spoke of earlier are not minor problems, but I suggest matters of State."

"Please, sir, I beg of you. I cannot deny your observations are correct, but these are troubled times; in Paris there is talk of revolution."

"Revolution, Monsieur!"

"Quietly, I beg of you."

"Pardon me, Monsieur, but I had no idea matters had reached such a terrible state."

"You are quite right, and I feel I must entrust in part some of my affairs, since I can see you are a man who is not easily fooled, and you are rather a friend than an enemy. I have papers upon my person which, if they fell into the wrong hands, would not only destroy my life, but perhaps hundreds of others. As soon as I reach England, I need to ensure these papers reach no lesser person than Lord Russell, the Prime Minister. I therefore entreat you, sir, to say nothing of this to a soul. Please, sir, go on with your story, as it intrigues me. You were saying that your servant had come across this lady that so entranced you."

"Indeed, Monsieur, the noise at the inn, as I had implied, was of the arrival of the young lady. My servant was by this time sure it was the lady he was looking for, since all her conversations were by use of her hands and the beguiling eyes. She did not seem to speak, and therefore he felt he must have at last found the women I sought.

"There was not much to be discovered that night, as she retired straight away to bed after the initial commotion. However, my servant, being warned she may leave as quickly as she had come, was up at first light. He then went to the stables to find that the horses were already being prepared for her carriage. To gain favour with a servant of hers who had been given the task of ensuring a speedy passage, he pretended to find a loose nail in a foreleg shoe. The servant was most appreciative, and during the episode gave up much about his mistress, although he himself had only been in her employ for three months. Her precise position in society was not known even to him, but it seemed she was forever meeting people of some considerable rank in society, both clergy and State. She seems to be entrusted with various matters, yet it was never clear where any of the related papers may be kept."

"And her name, sir? What was her name?"

"Her Christian name seemed to be Ann, but the name placed in the visitors' book kept by the innkeeper was probably false, since my servant surreptitiously followed her, and at each stop, one of four of five names was used. He did discover that other men who paid her attention always seemed to be visiting her when the moon was nearly full. He discovered this by accident, first noticing on three occasions when arriving at Calais that the tide was at its most beneficial for an immediate departure across La Manche. However, on a further occasion when the moon was full, she was instead near Paris, but nevertheless a gentleman of similar build to one he had seen elsewhere was in her presence, although he could not give a very good description as he was viewing from a distance.

"Looking back at this, I see that when she glanced up at me in the bedroom, she may in fact have been looking at the moon, which as I remember was not quite full, but would have been the next day. Thus, perhaps she was concerned she must get some rest if she was to be at Calais at her appointed time. With this pattern of events established, my servant returned to me and, not wishing to arouse suspicion, I now became the detective. You may have noticed that the moon is nearly full; indeed, it will be so tomorrow night. I have discovered that she will be taking a cabin on a small boat, *La Petite Fleur*, on the evening tide. There is only one other cabin and I mean to be in it. But you, sir, how do you intend to cross La Manche?"

"Why, on the same boat!"

"This is indeed fortuitous, Monsieur, but how do you say, things get ahead of me? No, this would be impertinent of me. I could not ask; I must trust to events."

"You sound, sir, as if you are trying to concoct some plan. What were you thinking? Were you going to suggest I share your cabin? I would be happy to pay my share of the cost."

"Ah yes, Monsieur. I mean no. Well, to be honest, I was a little hopeful in my thoughts; how you English say 'daydreaming'. I was trying to think of a way to be in her favour. You see, she will be in one cabin, and you and I in the other, but how to meet on favourable terms? How to get an introduction? If one could contrive to create a scene in which I could intercede."

"You mean if I could perhaps try and force my affections on this lady, and you come to the rescue? Ha, ha. We English, sir, even our women need more subtlety. No, you will have to gain your own favours, although from your story she is still in your debt. Nevertheless, I will do you a service and I will introduce her to you during the journey, let us say one hour after we have left port. If you think she is English by birth, I should have no trouble in introducing myself. It would be more reasonable for her to allow me to speak to her, do you not think?"

"Well, yes, it is possible. Although after all this time she must have picked up some French to be accepted by so many people this side of La Manche."

"Don't worry, sir, no English woman has outwitted me before. I'm sure you will find an introduction waiting for you. Trust me, sir. One hour after leaving port."

"Well, merci, Monsieur, if you are sure. I will always be in your debt."

"Think nothing of it, my dear sir. Now, I am tired, so I shall bid you bonne nuit, Monsieur."

"Et vous, Monsieur."

The two gentlemen retired to bed, but both were up early, anxious to ensure that they were on their way as soon as carriages and horses would allow. Although they acknowledged each other, neither said more than a word to the other. It was as if the night before had been a dream.

# Chapter 2

# The Rescue

The Englishman was away first, but set off in the opposite direction towards Paris, rather than Calais. *Perhaps*, thought the Frenchman, *he had some business elsewhere to attend to before travelling to the coast.*

In due course the Frenchman was seated in his carriage. "Allez nous."

"Oui, Monsieur Perevade," replied the coachman.

The coach rumbled out of town, and after about ten miles reached the bridge that was under repair. As they came upon it, there was a scene of much commotion. The local Magistrate, a surgeon, and what must be most of the local population, were gathered around. There was much agitation and toing and froing.

"Quel problème? Pouvons nous passe?" enquired Monsieur Perevade.

"Non, Monsieur, le pont est tombé."

The Frenchman was a little troubled at this news, but as he began to hear the full details, he got out of his coach to see if he could help. Apparently, while the workmen were repairing the bridge, a section of wall had collapsed into the water, taking two men with it and trapping them. They had not been killed, but the huge stones had pinned the men's legs to the riverbed. Fortunately, it was at the edge where the water was no more than half a metre deep, but they could only breathe with difficulty and were being held above water by their fellow workers.

The huge pieces of wall must have weighed over two tons, and although the men had managed to tie a cradle of ropes around and under the piece of wall, even with 20 men struggling in the water, they could not move it. In fact, their struggling merely served to make both trapped men sink further into the mud.

Monsieur Perevade had some knowledge of engineering, and studied the problem from a distance. Any attempt to raise a scaffold on the structure was likely to bring more bridge down. And a tripod in the water was not possible, as one leg would have to be in the much deeper, fast running channel, where the bottom of the river was deep clay. This would mean the leg was likely to sink into the clay as soon as any effort was made to raise the piece of wall.

He wandered over to a small ale house beside the bridge to give the problem some more thought, and was tapping out his pipe on an empty barrel when the answer came to him.

"Vite, vite!" he shouted. "Portez les barils, aussi une pompe et des tubes."

The hubbub stopped and the workmen, seeing the possible advantage, did as he requested. Floating the barrels into the water, they started to attach the ropes.

"Non, non. Renvoyez l'air et rejoignez les tubes et la pompe. Sous l'eau, alors la cordage."

"Mais, Monsieur, Nous ne comprenons pas."

The workmen were puzzled, as they did not see how two barrels full of water, tied each side of the section of wall, would help. However, Monsieur Perevade was most insistent, so they did what he said. Then, with two men holding the pump, and a third providing action, slowly the barrels were refilled with air and the water expelled. As if by magic, the ropes became taught and the trapped men, who had almost given up hope of rescue, began to cry out excitedly as the weight on their trapped legs began to grow less. After a few minutes their fellow workers were able to drag the men free. A great cry went up from the assembled throng as the men were carried to the riverbank.

The Magistrate, who had been all bluster, ran up to Monsieur Perevade and hugged him. "Merci, Monsieur, maintenant mon neveu vivra."[1]

Monsieur Perevade accepted the thanks from the two injured men; even the man who needed a splint for a broken leg was most grateful.

Monsieur Perevade then mentioned to the Magistrate that he needed to be in Calais that evening, and taking another route might mean he would miss the tide.

The villagers were quick to respond. It gave them an opportunity to pay their debt of gratitude, and it seemed most were in some way related to the two rescued men. Thus, they set about taking some part of Monsieur Perevade's luggage from the coach and carrying it across the bridge. Then the now lightened coach was carefully guided across the bridge by a dozen men, checking at each stage that it was not in danger of toppling into the river. Once safely across, the luggage was stowed aboard the coach again and Monsieur Perevade was sent on his way with much cheering, more thanks, and several bunches of flowers, hastily put together by the young girls of the village.

The rest of the journey proved uneventful and on arrival at the dock he soon found *La Petite Fleur*. On boarding the boat, he noticed a couple of small trunks, stowed aft, of a style suggesting they belonged to a lady. He was thus confident the woman he

---

[1] Thank you, Monsieur, now my nephew will live.

sought was already aboard. He paid the boat owner, who was also the captain, a portion of the fare to ensure there was fresh food and wine. He then went below to his cabin, having explained to the captain that he had agreed to share it with an Englishman whom he had expected to be aboard already, but there was no sign of him.

The tide had already started to turn, and he became anxious that the Englishman might miss his passage. The wind also took up and waves began to lap against the boat, but only enough to give the vessel a gentle rocking motion.

Monsieur Perevade decided to lie down in his bunk, more from feeling tired than from the rocking motion. But after all the excitement of the day, he began to relax, and it was not long before he fell asleep.

## Chapter 3

# "I'm afraid there are no roses."

It was sometime later that Monsieur Perevade awoke with a start, when the cabin boy opened the door in a rather clumsy and noisy manner, bringing a bottle of wine and some bread and cheese.

"Eh, merci," he said out of politeness, although he was a little annoyed at being woken so abruptly, then dismissed the boy with a wave of his hand. He looked around. *Where is the Englishman?* he wondered. Then he realised from the sound of the waves and the motion of the boat that they had put out to sea.

The same feeling of disappointment spread over him as had done on being dismissed by the lady 'Ann'. He poured himself some wine and considered how he might contrive a reason to enter her cabin, when suddenly the door opened again and in walked the Englishman.

"Sacré bleu, vous êtes arrivé. Mais quand?"[2]

"Oh, Monsieur Jean, I have been elsewhere on the boat, but I will explain all. Come, I promised you an introduction and would have done so on leaving port, but you were in such a deep sleep I did not like to wake you."

"You know my Christian name then?"

---

[2] Good heavens, you have arrived. But when?

"Oh yes, and a lot more besides, but all will become clear shortly. I am Richard Carlton, by the way. Now, we are about an hour off Newhaven, and I need to fill you in, as all is not what it seems. I contrived to wake you by asking the cabin boy to be rather noisy, so do not be too hard on him."

"Yes, he did startle me at first, but the wine was welcome."

"Now follow me."

Monsieur Perevade followed the Englishman out of the cabin and as he did so, spied the bouquets of flowers given to him that morning. He quickly grabbed a small bunch.

"In here, sir. Après vous."

Jean entered slowly. All these months of waiting... and now! He stepped forward, and there she was, dressed in sombre clothes, yet still with those captivating eyes that left the Frenchman temporarily speechless. It was as though he had suddenly become a shy, young teenager.

"Monsieur Perevade, je suppose," she said, with a delightful chuckle in her voice. "Mon mari Richard m'a tout dit sur vous."[3]

"Votre... votre mari!"[4] he replied in disbelief.

Then Ann continued in English to ensure Richard knew what was being discussed.

"I'm afraid so. I think I see a little disappointment in your face, but can we at least be friends?" She held out her small, artistic hand.

Monsieur Perevade hesitated then slowly took it and kissed it with such reverence that she was for a moment entranced by him. Regaining her composure, she said, "Do you by chance have a twin brother, or perhaps a cousin?"

---

[3] My husband Richard has told me all about you.
[4] Your... your husband!

Monsieur Perevade was taken aback by this question. "Yes, I have a twin brother, but how did you know? I have not seen or heard from him for years. It would not surprise me if he was dead."

Jean said the last word with a tone of expectation or hope that he was dead.

The young lady noticed this and, picking up on it, said, "Do I take it you would wish your brother was dead?"

"He is a rogue, a thief, a liar, and almost certainly a murderer. Since we were born, it is as if he had the devil in him. When we were children, I suffered at his hands on many occasions. He would do things, dastardly things, and then prey on our blood relationship to give him an alibi. The last occasion this occurred was some years ago… a terrible affair. A young girl was raped and murdered, and when suspicion fell on him, he pretended to be me and produced several witnesses that swore he was elsewhere. I was in Italy at the time on business and, being away for several months, knew nothing of the matter until my return. By that time, it was too late and he had disappeared."

"Well," she said, slumping down on the bunk, and as if the words would choke her added, "that girl was my sister!"

"Oh no," whispered Monsieur Perevade. "C'est terrible."

"Don't upset yourself, my dear." The Englishman put his arm around his wife's shoulder. "Let me tell the rest of the story."

Monsieur Perevade was shocked and even embarrassed at this revelation. Finding he still held the small bouquet of flowers, he gently held it out to her. "I'm afraid no rose this time," he said.

She looked up at him with a slight smile, and took the flowers without a word.

"You must forgive my wife, but the matter still affects her so."

"No, no. It is I who should be begging for forgiveness. I would guillotine my brother myself if I thought it would bring your wife's sister back."

"The truth is," began the Englishman, "my wife discovered her sister moments after the terrible event. It was not just that she had been raped and strangled, but her body had been mutilated in indescribable ways. The shock was such that she was struck dumb, and it took her some months to recover and regain her speech. She found that for dumb people, others think you are also deaf. In the process, she learnt to lipread, and while in her 'solitary confinement', as it were, she began to observe people more and noticed how you can tell what people are saying as much by their attitude and expression of hands and face as the words themselves."

Monsieur Perevade interjected, "This is true. In recent months I also found this when searching for a clue to your wife's whereabouts. But forgive my interruption, please go on."

"Well, sir, I am an Ambassador, and I need eyes and ears everywhere in these troubled times. With my wife playing dumb, she is accepted as French one day and English the next, merely by the choice of her clothes and a few mannerisms. As she never speaks, she never gives away that she is really from southern France."

"C'est fascinant, Monsieur, but I still do not see why – knowing what you do about me – you have let me come on this boat. Why did you not tell me at Estrée-Blanche?"

"Because, sir, in recent years my wife has been on the trail of your brother. When you appeared to assist her all those months ago by paying the insistent coachman, she could not believe you could be your brother. But she was obviously shocked and puzzled because you look so alike."

"Ah, I see now why she looked so worried when I entered her bedroom."

"You did not realise how close you came to being shot, as under the bedclothes was a loaded revolver. The presenting of the rose probably saved your life. The two actions of generosity and charm were so out of character with your infamous brother that Ann decided there must be two of you. However, I felt it better to bide our time, as I was not sure until now that you might not warn your brother of our interest in him."

"Sacré bleu, then your wife must have thought for a time that I was going to rape and kill her. C'est terrible. Mon Dieu, I shiver at the thought of it. But you say you have been searching for my brother, do you know where he is?"

"Why, yes. He should meet us at Newhaven. Although, you understand, he is expecting to be paid for something of value belonging to my wife's family. May I ask, sir, if you wear something unusual in your hat?"

"Well, yes. A brooch, which as you will recall was given to me by the young lady… I mean, your wife."

"Then, sir, continue to do so. If we have any problems in separating you two at Newhaven, it might be your salvation, as the rose was before. My wife deliberately gave you the brooch as a test. You see, your brother – he calls himself Count Dumas, by the way – almost certainly stole an identical brooch from Theresa, Ann's sister. And she knew when you accepted it so graciously, and with a puzzled expression on your face, that you could not possibly be Dumas, as any hint of recognition would have given the game away. And as for displaying it, well, that would be tantamount to pleading guilty. Yet you have no reservations about wearing it."

"Ah, now I begin to comprehend the events of that night. But you will forgive me, sir, if I remove it from my hat and put it below my lapel. You see, if my brother should see me wearing it, he might suspect something. Whereas, if it is a case of quickly recognising who is who, I will only have to finger my lapel surreptitiously, and someone like you can see who is who. My brother was always a master at imitating me, and knowing how his mind works, it will take only a few minutes for him to convince any unsuspecting soul that he is me, Jean, and that we must track down the infamous brother Philippe. And before you know it, I shall be the one the Magistrate has in irons. Even our voices sound alike, although when he laughs, he has the habit of hissing through his teeth."

"Very well. I agree, but we shall clearly need to be on our guard."

Ann had by now become more composed, and she interjected, "Yes, I see we shall need a password. I suggest, 'I'm afraid there are no roses'."

At this they all laughed, and Richard poured them each a glass of wine. "Let us drink to a new friendship, et le piège."[5]

"Oui, très bon," said Ann, with a smile.

"I am still a little puzzled, though," said Jean. "Why all this trouble to retrieve a brooch, if you have just given its duplicate away? I can easily return this one with pleasure."

"Ah! I had not finished. You see, it is not the brooch that is of value, but a ring he also stole, which bears a family crest. Your brother also stole some letters signed by Ann, and he has been forging letters of credit and presenting these as genuine. As the letters are sealed with the family crest, my wife's bankers, who have an office in Canterbury, have been paying out large sums of money, totally unaware. For various reasons we do not wish to go to the bankers and advise them to refuse payment, particularly as those who are finally encashing these bills may be

---

[5] And the trap.

innocent parties. My situation means that I must be seen to be beyond reproach, and any doubt over my credibility would be a serious hindrance.

"We have, therefore, agreed through a rather unlikely intermediary to provide a large sum of gold and a passage to Spain in return for the ring. However, I hold in my pocket a warrant for the arrest of your brother on a charge of murder. He will, we hope, come on board this boat in the belief that it is his passage to Spain. We even have some gold which I hope will be enough to entice him on board to take possession of the rest, which we will say is stored in this cabin. You will note, however, that the portholes are all barred. And once inside this cabin, it will become his prison."

*Chapter 4*

# At the Pilgrim

In Newhaven it had been a blustery night, and it would be several hours before the first light of dawn could be appreciated, especially as the drizzle that had been falling continued to blow in the stiff breeze.

A few fishermen were on the quay checking their tackle, but otherwise all was quiet. The harbour light was barely visible, obscured by the drizzle and a bank of mist that was being blown off the sea. The only noise heard above the general swish of waves breaking against the landing stages was the clink of shackles and rigging as the boats in the harbour jostled against their moorings.

In the town at the Pilgrim Inn a few men sat, still drinking and joking at four in the morning. A thick-set man was cajoling his followers to swallow up and drink yet again to his new wealth, as today his ship would come in.

Most of the party were hangers-on, happy to accept the bounty of free beer and wine, and the occasional bowl of stew from a huge pot that hung over an open fire like a witch's cauldron. Only one of the parties knew that the ship contained gold, although a couple of others who had known their 'benefactor' for some time, were suspicious that there was more to this ship than met the eye. They doubted if it really would be coming from the Indies; after all, most ships from those parts of the world tied up at Bristol, or possibly Liverpool.

Why struggle up the Channel to Newhaven before discarding its cargo of sugar or tobacco? Indeed, Bristol was the place where they knew how to turn tobacco leaves into a usable product. No, there had to be something special on this boat, if one existed, and by the money that had been spent that night, it was going to be far more valuable than the silver the landlord had been given to keep the revellers well supplied with wine and vitals.

"You see that silver moon? Well, to me it is golden," Dumas joked to the company, who by now laughed on cue.

"Bless you, master, may all your blessings turn to gold."

"Oh, they will," said the portly man, and thumped his hand again on the table. "Plus de vin ici, landlord, you old skinflint. Where are the bottles of wine I paid you for?"

"Drunk, sir."

"Why do you say drunk?"

"Why, see here, sir – the empty bottles."

"Well, we had better have two more." With that, two more florins came out of a deep pocket and were thrust into the landlord's hand. "Now, where's that boy of yours?"

"In bed, sir."

"Then get him out. I've a job for him, as there's a shilling to be earned. Now tell him to go up to the harbour and tell me the moment a boat arrives in the name of *La Petite Fleur*."

"But it's four-thirty in the morning, sir!"

"I know what time it is, and I say he goes to the harbour. How much have I paid you this night, and you're quibbling over getting the boy up early? He needs discipline, sir. Now get him up the harbour 'vite', or I take my business elsewhere."

The landlord reluctantly withdrew, produced the extra bottles, and then went to wake his 12-year-old son. It took a full thirty minutes to rouse the boy and have him dressed to send on his mission. Once he was awake enough to take in the message, the boy gratefully accepted the possibility of gaining of a shilling. After all, a shilling simply to report when a ship arrived in the dock seemed more than fair pay. The boy enjoyed being down on the docks and was no stranger to the fishermen thereabouts. So, he scurried off to see if a new ship was tied up and was soon chatting to a couple of regulars who were preparing their boats for the day's fishing.

"Any news of a boat called *La Petite Fleur*?"

"Why, I've not seen her hereabouts for a couple of weeks, but the moon's full, so she may well come in on the tide this morning. Why's a young chap like you so interested in a ship like her? She's no clipper, you know."

"Cos I've to earn a shilling by reporting back to the Count."

"What's Dumas up to now? One of his schemes, no doubt. Well, if she comes in, she be making for the north steps."

There were several berths along the wharf between the south and north steps. Only small boats could be accommodated at the north end, but at that location the larger ships were in danger of grounding even with a good tide.

The boy went back to the north steps, but the berth was empty and there was no sign of any new ship arriving since the evening before.

Unbeknown to Sam, another pair of eyes was measuring the tide and quietly mending nets. He saw the boy wander up and look about and then out to sea.

The observer was a semi-retired magistrate who occasional indulged himself in a little fishing while his health held out. His father had been a fisherman, and although he had spent many profitable years 'in court', he still yearned for a good breeze and the smell of the sea, that seemed to be in his bones.

*Dumas has sent a spy*, he thought. Although he recognised the boy was probably an innocent party, it showed that Dumas was obviously already suspicious about being paid off and closing his current source of wealth.

The man knew well enough that Dumas was a rogue, and he had willingly been recruited by the smartly dressed gentleman from London who had knocked on his door when he was still in office.

Just as the boy was about to turn tail, he thought he spied a light out to sea. So, he tarried a while in a doorway out of the wind and drizzle. Eventually a small boat came into view and, as expected, sailed up to the north steps and was soon tied up.

The boy was about to run home to deliver the news when he realised there may be more information the Count might want, such as what she was carrying, or who was on board.

On closer inspection the boy read the name 'La Petite Fleur' quietly to himself, and he was now confident that she was the right boat.

He looked the vessel up and down and quickly surmised that she must have just come across the Channel. There seemed almost no crew; just one lad to tie her up. She certainly had not come from the Indies. Few ships that arrived in Newhaven came from anywhere further afield than the Channel ports like Cherbourg, but rarely Spain or Holland.

The passengers of *La Petite Fleur*, if any, seemed in no hurry to disembark, so Sam prepared to go and tell the Count the news, but halfway back to the Pilgrim, curiosity got the better of him. If he could just see some of the passengers, perhaps he might be able to give the Count a fuller report; after all, was it actually a person the Count was expecting, rather than cargo?

The boat was high in the water and obviously not carrying anything in her small holds. Sam turned and, almost on tiptoe, retraced his steps back towards the dock. As he turned the last corner, he almost walked into a large, portly man, his cloak about him, with a hat well down to keep the drizzle out.

As the boy checked his step, he looked up at the man blocking his path, and a light from a nearby warehouse fell on the face of the stranger. Sam almost jumped backwards in surprise and embarrassment.

He cried out in a disconcerted tone, "It's at the north steps. I was just coming to tell you." Then, feeling foolish that he must have taken so long that Dumas had come down to look for himself, the boy ran off back home.

A few minutes later, out of breath from running all the way, he stumbled into the Pilgrim and met his father in the kitchen.

"Well?" said his father. "Is the boat in?"

"Yes," he said, "but I wasn't that long. I had to wait a bit before she came in. Why did the Count come down himself to see, anyway?"

His father ignored this last remark and said, "Go and tell the Count straight away."

"I told him down at the dock."

"What do you mean? Go and tell the Count. He's still drinking in the bar, so go and tell him before he gets angry."

"But I told him once!"

"Just go in and tell him, or you'll not get that shilling," his father warned.

The boy hesitated then sheepishly entered the bar.

"Well, boy, what news?" asked the Count.

"I've told you down the dock, the boat's in. You saw her."

"What are you mumbling about, boy? I sent you on an errand and am paying good money. Is she in or not?"

"She's in. I told you down the dock."

"I've been sat here. Do you think I'd be paying you to tell me, if I were going myself? If I have a dog, I don't expect to bark myself."

The assembled company laughed at this and joined the questioning.

"Eh, boy, how big is this ship, eh? Three masts, four? What's she carrying?"

"She's only small, and probably came across the Channel. I don't know what she has. Anyway, the Count saw her."

"Why do you keep saying I been down the dock, boy?"

"Because I nearly bumped into you, just by the corner of the road to the dock."

"Well, it was not moi, unless I have a double."

The followers laughed again and interjected, "How many Count Dumas do you think there are, boy?"

But at this, Dumas was already starting to frown. "What did this chap look like, the one you say was me?"

"Well, he was heavy built like you, and same height."

"What was he wearing?"

"A cloak and hat, a hat like the one there." The boy pointed to the hat of French style lying on the bench close by. "And he had a beard like yours, although perhaps it was neater."

"Anything else, boy?"

"He got your nose."

"Jean," said Dumas under his breath.

He beckoned the boy closer and said quietly, "Tell me, boy, what did this man say? And for that matter, what did you say to him?"

"I said only that the boat was in at the north steps. He didn't say anything. Anyway, it was definitely you, so why are you asking all these questions?"

"Now listen here, boy," Dumas bent down to talk directly to the boy so that the company would not hear, "whoever you saw, you keep it to yourself, do you understand? Now here's that shilling I promised you, and here's another. You go and keep watch, and if this man you say was me comes anywhere near the Pilgrim, you come straight back here to tell me. But this is the important bit. When you come back, you hold out the shilling and I'll exchange it for a florin. Do you understand what I say, boy? No mistakes this time."

The boy nodded excitedly. Two shillings already before breakfast was a fortune, and he was anxious to please.

"Where will you be?" he asked.

"I'll be here, or in my room. Et one more thing. If you come and see me, and I do not offer to give you a florin, tu conserves ta bouche fermée, et alors tu skedaddle; tu comprends,[6] boy?"

"Yes, Mr Dumas."

The boy went out into the kitchen, grabbed a slice of bread and a piece of cheese, then took his coat and went out the back door, mumbling to himself that he was hunting for the "other Dumas".

Meanwhile, on *La Petite Fleur*, Richard had seen the brief exchange between Monsieur Perevade and the boy.

"What did the boy want, Monsieur Perevade?"

"Well, I think we may have a problem!" he replied.

"What, already!" The Englishman said this half joking, thinking there couldn't be anything to be concerned about yet!

However, Monsieur Perevade continued, "The boy said she's at the north steps. I was just coming to tell you. But he was obviously surprised, to say the least. I could see in his eyes that he seemed to recognise me, yet he was also puzzled. I think Dumas – my brother, that is – is ahead of us. That boy was sent as a scout, but thought I was Dumas. No doubt my brother, being quick-witted as well as cunning, may be suspicious that I am *'en ville'* – in town, that is; as you English say."

---

[6] You keep your mouth closed and then you skedaddle; you understand?

"This could prove awkward."

"Maybe, but the boy did not see us together, so even if my brother thinks I'm around, he may not expect my presence has anything to do with your arrival. That said, he may be thinking it can be no coincidence. Still, we will have to hope he considers it is just that. Perhaps, though, we can use this to our advantage. Suppose I seem to be bartering for the gold and Dumas's spies, or the boy, sees this, what do you think would happen?"

"I'm confused," said Richard. "Why should you barter for the gold?"

"No reason, but my brother won't know that. He will just see his wealth floating away!"

"You mean if he thought the gold was on the boat, he might try and retrieve it?"

"Something like that. But how to portray this charade in such a way that it portrays the right message to the right people? Le problème: who are my brother's friends? I use the word 'friends' loosely, and who might be people who by now he owes more than just a favour?"

"Well, I may be able to help you there. I have my spies as well. You see the white house, up high on the east side of the harbour?"

"Oui."

"Well, that is the home of a semi-retired magistrate, a certain Lawrence Courtney. I have engaged him to find out all he can about Dumas. He was very willing to help, as Dumas has appeared in his court several times, but each time witness alibis would appear as if by magic and charges that seemed cut and dry just faded away so he was forced to release your brother."

"That sounds like my brother, making sure someone else gets the blame," Jean said, as much to himself.

"Let us go and talk to him. Come, we can take this rowboat."

And with that the company climbed into the boat, untied it, and pushed off across the harbour. Only Ann remained behind, ready to signal should any danger appear.

## Chapter 5

# The Plan

It only took a few minutes to cross the harbour and wander up to the Magistrate's house. The company were a little surprised when a voice came from behind them.

"I saw you crossing and recognised you; I've been keeping an eye on matters, as I promised. There is no mistaking you, Monsieur Perevade. You are the spitting image of your brother! The boy seemed to get a shock when he bumped into you, sir. Indeed, I have to keep reminding myself you are the good guy, as you certainly are extraordinarily alike. Indeed, if I had not been forewarned that you might be aboard, I would be believing Dumas was already all but captured."

"If I did not know I would be accompanying Mr Richard ici, how did you?"

"Oh, we've been planning this for some time; your interest in Ann has been noted for some months. We perhaps had the advantage of realising there might be two of you, since your brother – I assume he is your brother – could not be on both sides of the Channel at once."

"It seems you English have been planning all this, and there I was thinking I was so clever just tracking Mademoiselle Ann down." At this Jean Perevade laughed, but realising his voice may carry, he cut short his chuckling and said, "Perhaps we should go inside, only there seem to be more spies around than people."

Indoors, it was immediately quieter out of the breeze and drizzle, as well as a little warmer. They stood in a small, snug room, where a stove threw out welcome heat to dry off the assembled trio.

"Gentlemen, a drink." The Magistrate produced glasses and a bottle of wine.

"Thank you," said the visitors together.

"Here, let me take those cloaks, and come sit by the fire."

They gathered about the stove and supped their wine.

"Well, what news of Dumas? Is he still spending freely?"

"Oh yes, he spreads his largess about to all and sundry. If this goes on, shopkeepers will be putting their prices up to cope with demand."

"If that is true, we need to act swiftly. My wife's family are rich, but not that rich!"

"Well, maybe I'm exaggerating a little, but it seems like that sometimes. Although, it does seem he's upset a couple of people, and one in particular. Apparently, there was a late-night card game some three weeks ago, which ended up with just two of them bidding. When the cards were turned, Dumas lost, wrote out an I.O.U. and has failed to honour it. He is now trying to make out the game was fixed against him. The person concerned was the local butcher – a person you would not wish to meet on a dark night. Indeed, only someone like Dumas would think of crossing this guy, who could easily break your neck like he was despatching one of his chickens.

"Dumas keeps saying he will pay, but then makes excuses. However, I note Dumas now keeps with his own followers and is rarely seen alone, so that our butcher cannot apply a little persuasion for early payment."

There was a pause, then Jean Perevade spoke slowly as he formulated his idea.

## La Nuit à Therouanne

"If we say that I met him – this butcher – and suggested I can now pay him, in front of this boat, and news got back to my brother, what would he do?"

"Wouldn't Dumas think you are bailing him out again?" asked the Magistrate.

"Not if it was made clear that *La Petite Fleur* was carrying the gold that I was now able to pay him with."

"But didn't you say you did not want Dumas to know that you had any connection with us and *La Petite Fleur*."

"Yes, I did, but no matter. As I see it, thinking like my brother, he is going to suspect every action you or I take. Firstly, we need to send a message to this butcher fellow, preferably using the boy that bumped into me. Do we know his name?"

"Oh, that's young Sam, the Pilgrim Innkeeper's son," said the Magistrate. "That is where Dumas is holed up. I spied him there at midnight when I made a quick reconnoitre. He was drinking the night away, as he often does with his band of merry men, or should I say hangers-on. But explain how you think we might get Dumas on the boat, and especially down into a cabin?"

"Well, I must admit to thinking out loud a little, and there could well be holes in my method. But if I go across and find Sam, and tell him that I can now pay the butcher in gold and he should come to *La Petite Fleur* at a certain time say… erm, when is the next high tide?"

"About 5 o'clock this evening," said the Magistrate.

"So, I pass this message to Sam, and no doubt even a boy like that will have worked out there are two of us and rush to tell Dumas, who by now will have him 'on a string', so to speak. My brother asks, 'Have you told the butcher?' 'No,' says Sam, who is no doubt expecting to be rewarded by delivering the message first to him. So, *pas de problème*,[7] thinks my brother.

"However, meanwhile, we send another message to the butcher to be on board *La Petite Fleur* by 4 o'clock if he wants his debt paid and in gold. And this is, how you say, the clever part. We send another message purporting to come from the butcher, saying the price has gone up, but he will be on the boat as agreed at three.

"Dumas will then be totally confused and wonder how the butcher came by this information if he thought he had intercepted the message! Also, it will now be apparent that the butcher will be expecting payment and that no further delaying tactics are going to work."

"Wow, that is a plan-and-a-half," said Richard, then continued, "We are forgetting something. We need the ring off his finger; always assuming he has it on him."

"Oh," said Jean, "that's the good part. You know the value of the ring, but I very much doubt if anybody else does. No, it seems to me that if you have my brother, your credit is safe, whether he has the ring or not. Once captured, he cannot use it."

"That's true," pondered Richard. "But there still seem to be an awful lot of ifs and buts, and I still do not see what is going to get Dumas on this boat."

"Well," said Jean, "let me continue with my plan, as I see it. If I think like my brother, I am surprised and suspicious that there is a plot forming about me, but equally I cannot afford to let the butcher on the boat, or all the gold may walk away from me. So, I either need to intercept the butcher – and from the sounds of it I would not want to do that, as otherwise the next thing I'd see is a meat clever – or I need to get there before

---
[7] Not a problem

## La Nuit à Therouanne

the butcher, which means possibly visiting Madam Ann, or yourself, and ingratiating myself with perhaps the production of the ring."

"Ah," said Richard, "I see how your mind is working. Double jeopardy: damned if he does, and damned if he doesn't."

Jean continued, "My guess is my brother will want the gold so much that he will come. Equally, he may try and take over the boat – that is, as long as he is sure there is indeed gold on the boat."

"Wait a minute," said the Magistrate. "If we tell the butcher the payment will take place elsewhere – after all, the butcher knows nothing of the boat so far – and then this fact is leaked to Dumas, Dumas would assume the gold is being moved. Thus there is no point in his band of cronies taking over the boat. We need to make it a place familiar to the butcher. That way Dumas's band may think twice about depriving him of payment. Most of his crew seem pretty weak and will not want to cross the butcher without good reason."

"Perhaps this is getting too complicated," said Jean. "Can we just take the easy course – go to the Pilgrim and arrange to offer gold for the ring?"

There was a moment of quiet as the company thought through all the scenarios and how any party might react.

"Well," said Richard, "we might get the ring that way, but of course, not Dumas for murder. What will Dumas do once he has the gold?"

"Skip town, I shouldn't wonder," said the Magistrate. "Perhaps hire a boat. Of course, the boat to hire would or could be *La Petite Fleur*, and if the gold did not have to move then, hey presto, gold and passage all in one go."

"So," said Richard, "we are back to the boat being the scene of make or break, us or him! However, if he did try and take the boat, we might persuade the captain of the frigate further seaward to fire a small broadside to dissuade him from leaving dock!"

"Well, gentlemen, I think this is a problem that needs some thought, and as between us we have not had much sleep, I suggest we retire and convene later."

"Why cannot I just arrest him?" asked the Magistrate.

"Unfortunately, the warrant is only valid in France," replied Richard.

"Does Dumas know that?" said the Magistrate, but then continued, "When I think of it, the Pilgrim is a bit of a rabbit warren. I cannot get enough men together to cover all the exits, especially as some of his men may put up a fight as well."

"I think as the next high tide is not until 5 o'clock this evening, we had best get some rest. Whichever plan we adopt, it can probably wait until midday. I cannot see Dumas hatching any plan of his own for a few hours at least."

"I agree," said the Magistrate. "There'll be fishermen down here in a couple of hours. This harbour can be quite busy early in the morning, so it's not the time to be a pirate."

The wine and warm fire meant that the thought of getting some rest was indeed inviting. So, the Englishman said he must return to Ann, and took the rowing boat back across to *La Petite Fleur*. They agreed to reassemble at 12 o'clock on the *Fleur* to decide what action to take.

For the next few hours, it was as if time stood still as far as *La Petite Fleur* and the Pilgrim were concerned. The boat party, after the discussions and wine, were glad to get some rest, as did those including Dumas, after consuming more wine than was good for him. Dumas realised something was afoot, but knowing the state of the tide and dock filling up with fisherman, this was not the time to be hijacking a boat for the want of gold.

## La Nuit à Therouanne

Thus, at midday, Ann and Richard Carlton welcomed Jean Perevade and the Magistrate, Lawrence Courtney, back onto *La Petite Fleur* as agreed.

"I have been thinking," said the Frenchman. "How you English say, not seeing the wood for the trees. If my brother was on his own, he could be overpowered and arrested by you, Magistrate, and a few of your fellow officials. The problem is getting all his followers to leave. But I can do that by simply telling them to go away, or at least sending them on some errand."

"True, if you were on your own and Dumas was elsewhere," agreed Richard. "But when could you be sure of meeting his merry band when Dumas was not present?"

"Ah, c'est le problème. I have not been thinking clearly," said Jean. "The key to the situation may be the boy Sam. We need to take him into our confidence. After all, he knows how many men Dumas can call upon and possibly what, if anything, Dumas has said of his forthcoming wealth."

"Is that not dangerous for the boy?" interjected Lawrence. "If Dumas thinks he is being double-crossed, the boy's life could be in danger."

"True. We will have to act very carefully," said Richard.

"Perhaps a woman's touch is required," interjected Ann. Although in the dark regarding all the earlier discussions and plans, she now saw how she might be of help. "If I struggle up the dock with a heavy bag, can we ensure the boy is nearby so I can ask for his help, and thereby gain an opportunity to befriend him?"

"No problem there. He tends to be in or about the dock all day at the moment, presumably to report back if something should happen," said Lawrence. "Also, I wonder if we are not trying to act too hastily. Do we have to return to France today?

If we leave it a bit, say until tomorrow's tide, this may unnerve Dumas and he may run out of funds and some of his followers may drift away."

"Is there a place nearby I might have a room other than the Pilgrim?" asked Ann.

"Why, yes," said Lawrence. "There is a coaching inn about a mile out, on the road towards Lewes."

"Then that could be ideal," said Ann. "It would give me plenty of time to win the boy over. Are there carriages about to hire for this trip?"

"The blacksmith at the corner of the dock may well be obliged to bring out his small trap for such a journey, if we make it worth his while," said the Magistrate.

"It seems we spend and spend. At least when this is all over, we can hopefully bring a halt to giving away all this money," said Richard, becoming a little frustrated.

"Don't worry, darling, let's take this one step at a time. As I see it, Dumas won't be rushing down to claim his prize; after all, he won't want anybody else to know about the gold. So, you go off to the blacksmith and get this trap ready, and as soon as it appears I'll get young Sam to help a pretty woman," she added with a laugh. The others smiled, appreciating that things had got a little over-complicated.

"Right, off you go, Richard. I'll expect a trap to appear by one o'clock."

## Chapter 6

# The Young Recruit

The weather had improved over recent hours, and this meant that when Richard started down the dock with the trap on loan from the blacksmith, it was quite bright with glimpses of the sun.

Ann was ready with her heavy bag and, looking about, soon spied young Sam. "Ici, boy, can you help me a moment?"

Sam was not one to miss a trick, as there might be tuppence in it, so he bounded over. "I'll carry that, Missus," he said.

"Well, Sam. It is Sam, isn't it? That would be most kind of you."

Sam was slightly taken aback about how this pretty lady knew his name, but the smile from her soon melted his heart, and he would have carried her bag the full mile to the coaching inn.

Richard pulled up a few yards in front of them.

"Now, place my bag in the back of the trap," said Ann.

Sam did so and was about take his leave when Ann took his arm. "Why, you are a strong lad. I need you for a short while. Now, this is my husband. Remember his face, as although he has business elsewhere, you may need to recognise him later. However, for now I need you to take the reins. Don't worry, lad, I am not kidnapping you – besides, you will have the reins. I need to be up at the coaching inn on the Lewes Road. Do you know it?"

"Well, yes," said Sam. "You mean the Red Post."

"Très bon, then it won't take us long and you can bring the trap back to the blacksmith. Can you do that for me, Sam? I will be most grateful." She put her arm round Sam and gave him a hug.

The young boy was suddenly feeling very important, being made up to 'coachman' for a lady of some style. Having dutifully loaded the carpet bag, he helped the lady Ann to the bench seat beside him, and with a quick flick of the reins he was off.

As they journeyed at a walking pace, avoiding odd crates of fish and other goods along the dock, Ann began to take Sam into her confidence.

"You seem to be good at handling horses, Sam."

"Well, yes," he said, "my father is the landlord of the Pilgrim, and I often put the horses into the stable. Just occasionally I put the horses into the traces and bring out a gentlemen's coach."

"I thought you had a good hand for horses," said Ann. "Do you by chance know a gentleman by the name of Count Dumas? He is staying at the Pilgrim."

"Yes," said Sam. "He's not very nice. I do not like him, although he gave me a shilling this morning, but I had to be up at the dock before it was light. Nobody likes him except all his cronies, but only because he has money, and I do not think the money is really his; he never does any kind of work. I know he owes lots to people. I think he owes the butcher, Mr Armstrong, some money. I had to take a note round there the other day and when the butcher read the note, he was not very pleased!"

"Well, Sam, I see you are a clever lad, and you are quite right not to upset Dumas. He is a thief, and even killed somebody."

"What, here in Newhaven?" asked Sam.

"No, in France," replied Ann, deciding not to tell Sam the whole story. "We need your help, Sam, but I expect you are bound to tell Dumas what is going on hereabouts."

"That's right. I am to look out for a man that looks just like him, and if I see him, I have to rush back and offer Dumas a shilling and he will give me two in exchange."

"A clever plan," Ann said quietly, more to herself than to Sam. "Well, I do not want you to get into trouble with Mr Dumas, so you do just what he told you. However, the man you bumped into on the dock early this morning was not Dumas."

"I thought it was odd Dumas should be checking on me. Who was he?"

"His name is Jean Perevade, and he is Dumas's identical twin brother."

"I have twin cousins, but you can easily tell them apart."

"Well," said Ann, "when two eggs grow inside a lady's womb at the same time, they are twins. But just occasionally, very early on in the lady's pregnancy, the one egg splits into two and that's when you get identical twins."

"So, what is this other guy doing here? Is he off to see his brother?"

"Ah well, Sam, if things were that easy. But we are trying to arrest Mr Dumas for the murder, but need to take him back to France for trial."

"Oh," said Sam, looking worried. "Am I in trouble then for helping him?"

"No, no, Sam, no-one's going to arrest you. We just needed to warn you, which is why I have got you holding the reins, which of course I could easily have taken myself. Now, as we are here at the Red Post, and by my reckoning you've had little to eat all day, come in and I'll get you some lunch."

"okay, but I better not be long, as if something happens back at the dock, Dumas will be annoyed at me not telling him."

"Don't you worry, young garçon, nothing will happen back at the dock yet. Maybe tomorrow morning. Now, I need you to be able to tell Dumas and his brother apart, especially in the dark. Monsieur Jean Perevade is more smartly dressed, but in the dark, or along a passageway in the Pilgrim, you may not have time to be sure. So, if you find yourself in an awkward situation and cannot tell them apart, then just say that there are no roses out in your garden."

"No roses? We don't even have a garden. Dumas will think I am nuts."

"Well," said Ann, "just say there are no roses out today. Even if Dumas thinks you are nuts, that is fine, but Mr Jean Perevade will catch on instantly and assist you. It saved his life once, and it might save yours."

"Weird," said Sam and chuckled, then he tucked into a tasty stew and dumplings that was set before him.

Before Ann left Sam to finish his lunch, she gave him one further instruction. "Be at the boat about one o'clock tomorrow morning, as we will need a message delivered."

Then, with a smile and a friendly hug, she went off to pay the landlord for a small room at the front of the Red Post, paying sufficient to cover both room and meals. She watched Sam leave the inn and take off in the trap at a good pace, confident that he would not only take his charge back to the blacksmith's stable but would be useful when the time came.

Back on board *La Petite Fleur*, they had decided a rush job was unnecessary and they would leave events until the next morning as Ann had anticipated.

At the Pilgrim, however, Dumas was becoming more unsettled and was pacing about. The landlord, Sam's father, was also becoming a little annoyed. He liked the man better when he just sat and drank, and of course paid for his wine and vitals. The hangers-on were also becoming less interested in staying around, and some wandered off to continue with some proper employment, if they had one. Most were just carters and were soon back to shifting wares around the harbour, or on carriages leaving for Lewes or Tunbridge Wells, or even London.

When Sam eventually put in an appearance, Dumas grabbed him by the scruff of the neck. "Where's you been these last hours? Is boat still at anchor? Who's aboard her?"

"She ain't moved, and there's two men plus the captain and his mate, but they've been down in the cabin all day. Otherwise, I ain't seen nothing."

"And this guy you say was me, have you seen him again?"

"I saw someone who had your build through a porthole window, but I could not be sure."

"Well, you're no good. No information, no money." Dumas then stomped off up to his small room at the back of the Pilgrim. The room was up two flights of stairs that allowed a quick exit, as he could step out of the window and onto a flat roof, and had been chosen deliberately in case of need.

Dumas lay on his bed to think. He realised something was up, as things were not going to plan. It had been agreed through covert messages that he would return the stolen ring as soon as the ship docked, in exchange for gold. However, while he had agreed to this some weeks ago, he had not really thought it through, and now he realised there must be some other motive – even though most of his crimes had been committed in France. He was pretty sure the return of the ring was a smokescreen, but he knew they could not arrest him here for French crimes, while the duping of a couple of drunken sailors of their bounty a few days ago would be of no consequence. He wanted to just march off down to the dock and do the business, but that was too easy. And anyway, if his brother was about, something else must be going on.

Dumas turned things over in his mind, then in frustration crept down to the dock after dark. *La Petite Fleur* was, as expected, tied up at the north steps. The glow of a lamp showed someone was in a cabin below, but otherwise all was quiet. Dumas was about to return to the Pilgrim when a face appeared out of the dark. Dumas, half recognised him as man who had been at the card game some weeks earlier.

"Why, Dumas, I hear you're into money. Off to pay Armstrong?"

"Ah, not quite. Just need to finish some business." Dumas rushed off feeling very vulnerable and annoyed he had been caught in the open without an escort.

He returned to the Pilgrim, ordered a stiff drink, and made light of things, gaining a small but not quite so enthusiastic audience. But they soon melted away when free booze did not seem to be the order of the day. Indeed, a few goaded him.

"This ship of yours in then? What's the cargo? When's pay day?"

Dumas growled and strode off up to his room. Matters were definitely not going to plan.

## Chapter 7

# The Waiting Game

The next day was Sunday, so the harbour was quiet. Also, it was a spring tide, so with the water falling more than normal boats were left settled at odd angles along the quayside, creating strange shadows as the bright sun moved across the sky. Gulls and terns made up a cacophony of sound echoing along the harbour wall. Nothing appeared to be amiss, and the tranquillity was hardly disturbed at all by the arrival of a lady on a horse, who pulled up opposite the *Fleur*. She dismounted and climbed on board, pulling open the hatch door that led below.

"Good morning," she said. "Any news?"

Ann advised that she had enjoyed a very restful night at the Red Post and some profitable conversations with a few Navy personnel who were billeted there. Her husband greeted her with a kiss and proceeded to update her.

"I have been quite busy myself," said Richard. "I have been walking around the dock, or drinking at the local pubs. Jean, not wanting to cause any further confusion, stayed on the boat with a loaded revolver to hand, just in case. There's much talk about Dumas and this butcher. It seems the whole town is either in one camp or the other, or perhaps just standing on the sidelines, but most have something to say on the matter and will regale you with almost no tempting. Most seem to know Dumas as a rogue, but none have listed his misdemeanours as murder. There is talk of him duping a couple of drunken sailors out of their bounty from a recent voyage. As for Armstrong the butcher, he seems to be keen on getting his payment, but is obviously a man who will strike when he sees fit and the opportunity is right."

"Well, Richard," said Ann, "on my way here this morning, who should I spy but young Sam. By the way, he has his head screwed on the right way and is quite mature for a boy of his age. He is primed to take any message we feel appropriate to Dumas, or Armstrong, or any others who may help our cause. He advised me that Dumas has been behaving strangely, pacing about or spending hours in his room. He's hardly drunk or eaten a thing, and it seems we were right to wait, as most of the men who were at his fingertips, having seen the true Dumas, have gone back to more honest trades.

"The best bit of information was what Sam told me about last night. That boy is a professional when it comes to spying! Apparently, he followed Dumas down here last night when dark. It seems Dumas wanted to check for himself if this boat was here and who was on board. Anyway, he saw the *Fleur* with a light below and, being on his own, proceeded no further. But then he turned to go back and, by chance, bumped into a gentleman in the butcher's camp. Sam was near enough to hear that the man said to Dumas something like 'Your ship's in then, when are you paying Armstrong?' and Dumas replied, 'When I've finished my business.' Then Dumas was back to the Pilgrim so fast that Sam had to run at top speed down the back alleys to be sure of being there first, so that Dumas would not suspect he had been out. Sam's face, as he told me, was quite a picture."

"Well," said Jean, "I think we better have a plan, as it seems my brother is on the back foot. We need your magistrate friend over here to give us authority. Do we ask the butcher to come here or elsewhere, with the news Dumas is offering to settle?

Apparently, the Captain says, with this wind the tide will not be right to leave till after 5pm, but once we set sail, we will make good speed to France. Where is young Sam at the moment?"

"I told him we may need him at about one o'clock," said Ann.

"Then let's prepare things below, check all the bars are fitted, and locks work. And where is this gold? My brother will be as suspect as a timid cat and be away in a moment if matters do not go according to his plan."

"You mean we need for it to look as if he is driving the business," said Richard.

"Absolutely," replied Jean.

The party set about ensuring everything was in its place. Ann, however, would not be going with them, so most of her things were already at the Red Post.

After about an hour the boat looked set, with an inviting small table set on deck with glasses and wine, as if this was to be a small business meeting and refreshments would be in order to seal the deal. They hoped this may also put the butcher and his band at ease.

The wording of the messages was proving difficult. There needed to be clarity, but also the need to sound honest and genuine, and perhaps contain some words that particularly Dumas would recognise so that he felt he had received a genuine message – not something that would trap him. They were just agreeing on the wording when there was a tap on the hatch door.

Richard was immediately suspicious and asked everyone to keep back. Taking his revolver, he moved to open the cabin door. Then, moving slowly, he carefully and quietly climbed the steps that led up to the deck, opening the hatch with a sudden deliberate movement to find young Sam standing there.

Sam was taken aback by this sudden movement and to find a revolver in his face.

"*Roses, red roses,*" he said.

"Sam, my dear lad, what are you doing here? We weren't expecting you for another hour. Come down quickly. What's the trouble? *Red Roses,*" Richard laughed. "You are well schooled then. Well thought out, my boy."

"I have to deliver a message," the boy blurted out.

"You have a message for us? From whom?"

"Dumas sent me, and I need to be back in 15 minutes, or there could be trouble. I don't know what trouble, although I think it may be something to do with fire, as he kept flicking matches into the fireplace in the parlour at the Pilgrim."

"Where's this message then?"

"Here." Sam handed across two bags and a message, then added, "I am to take back a reply."

"Ah," said Jean. "Never underestimate my brother. He must have realised we were playing a waiting game, so he has decided to move events on his terms."

Richard opened the message and read it out aloud. "Place £5 in gold in the green bag, and £60 in the red bag. Sam has the letters which he will surrender for the green bag. The ring I will bring at 4pm. Hang the red bag where I can see it near the gangplank. I am expecting a Mr Armstrong to call by, and I will settle my business with him before I come to the boat."

Richard looked grave. "That's £65 in gold for the ring; that was never the agreement."

"How much did you agree?" asked Jean.

"£50 in total."

"Well, we need to get ready with what we have got," said Jean. "But first, give Sam the £5 in gold. Now then, Sam, tell Dumas we agree. We cannot have you in trouble, but once you have delivered the message, make yourself scarce. There's something not right about this, but if we are quick and seem to be following his request, he will be less suspicious."

"I do not like giving up £5 in gold for these letters," warned Richard.

The Frenchman moved across to his English friend and spoke softly. "I dare say you are right, but we must keep ahead of things. If we seem to be stalling now, he may have us playing, how you say, 'cat and mouse' for days."

So, Sam was quickly dispatched with the green bag containing the requisite £5 in gold, and with strict instructions to then stay well away from the area. As the boy was about to leave the boat, Jean Perevade rushed after him.

"Sam, do you know if my brother has a gun?"

"Maybe," Sam replied with a shrug. "But I've not actually seen one."

"Right," said Jean. "Now, be off, et vite."

*Chapter 8*

# The Settlement

The time was about a quarter past twelve and Dumas was not due until four, so for the moment he still had the upper hand. Both Dumas and the party knew they could not sail for at least an hour after the agreed time, which meant that even if they got him on the boat, he would not need to be swimming ashore. Indeed, the whole business might only take a few minutes.

"Of course," said Jean Perevade. "The butcher. The butcher, how much was he owed? What was the bet?"

"I don't know," said Richard. "No-one I spoke to mentioned an actual figure. You think the £5 was really for the butcher?"

"Could well be, which means he may have grabbed young Sam on his return and simply sent him straight out again to settle with the butcher. Thus, in one stroke he has got rid of any interference, with the main settlement here at 4pm. Even if the amount owed is slightly more, the butcher may settle for the £5 rather than press the matter and cause an endless feud."

Richard was now pacing about the cabin. "Dumas has us just where he wants us. He has only to hold out the ring with one hand and expect us to drop this red bag full of gold in the other."

Jean, however, was not so anxious and calmly suggested that he should conduct the business on deck, where everybody could see what was going on. That way, his brother would not be so concerned about being caught, but could simply take flight back across the gangplank at a moment's notice, if he so wanted.

"You, just on your own? I'm not sure about this," said Richard, with a slight air of contempt in his voice. He had not brought Jean across the Channel to be a broker.

Ann had also been thinking the matter through.

"Actually, that may not be a bad idea," she said. "He is the only person that Dumas may just feel he can trust; after all, up until now he has relied on his brother to escape from all his previous problems. He may see Jean as a saviour. It may certainly help if we can get him aboard. After all, none of us saying 'please come aboard' is likely to get a positive response."

"Yes, you and Lawrence can be down here with your revolver, ready to spring into action as required," added Jean.

"Well, if there might be bullets flying about, you had better be ashore," Richard told his wife.

There was another tap at the hatch and a familiar voice rang out, "Can I come below?"

Lawrence Courtney, the retired Magistrate, entered the cabin.

"What news?" he asked. "I saw young Sam come aboard. Have you dispatched him with appropriate messages?"

"No, Dumas got here first… or at least his message did."

The party quickly brought Lawrence up to date.

"Jean thinks he alone should conduct the settlement," said Richard.

"Actually, that may not be a bad idea," mused Lawrence. "Two brothers enjoying a drink together is unlikely to attract attention, but Dumas skipping about in front of you, Richard, could turn a few heads."

Time was ticking on and Ann had taken her leave. But 4pm came and went, and just when they were thinking Dumas must have decided it was too risky, a small party arrived at the corner of the dock.

## La Nuit à Therouanne

The strong southerly wind, which would hold back the outgoing tide, continued to blow. As Dumas's party walked slowly towards the *Fleur*, it became apparent that they had been rather clever. For while Sam may have tried to make himself scarce, one of Dumas's men had effectively kidnapped the boy and now had him walking between two of Dumas's sturdy co-conspirators. With at least one hand always on the young lad's shoulder, they ensured that he could not make a run for it as they approached the boat.

The party, with Sam in the middle, stopped opposite the boat, leaning against some boxes while Dumas gingerly approached the *Fleur*.

Jean Perevade, who was seated on the deck as planned, immediately saw the dilemma they were in. Any attempt to capture Dumas would obviously be met with young Sam being threatened and could be used, if necessary, as an exchange hostage. Nevertheless, he held up a glass of wine to greet his brother.

"My dear Philippe, will you not take a glass of wine with me? Are we not born brothers?"

Dumas said nothing but slowly edged towards the red bag.

Suddenly the relative peace on the dock was broken when a small party of sailors appeared. Clearly worse for drink, they began walking along the dock.

Dumas realised his time was running out, but then thought that if he struck as the sailors passed, he could make off in the confusion.

However, he was not the only one to be anticipating the disturbance as the sailors were about to pass. Sam was not actually bound to either of his burly protectors, but he had feigned compliance with their wishes, knowing he could easily outrun them if necessary. He had also noted something that others not familiar with this dock would notice. The wind had dropped, and the tide was now starting to turn as it often did if the sun was shaded by increasing cloud. The other factor was one which only a young lad would appreciate and be practised at. If you wanted to take away any stolen item which a mate had cheekily lifted from the piles of goods lying about the dock, you could temporarily disable your fellow thief with a sharp blow to the calf muscles and liberate from him any item he had managed to purloin.

With a carefully planned move, Dumas stepped forward and grabbed the bag. Feeling it was heavy, and satisfied it contained gold, he turned to make his escape.

At that point, Sam pounced. He leapt forward, grabbing a chunk of wood he had been eyeing, and with a stroke worthy of a keen cricketer he whacked the rogue Dumas across his calf muscles. As anticipated, the man let out a yelp, cursing the lad, then fumbled and dropped the bag. Sam had been expecting this and he caught the booty, then with one swing sent the bag into the air and onto the deck near Jean Perevade.

For a moment all the parties were stunned by this interference, but soon realised the tables had been turned, not just the tide.

Richard, who had been watching the proceedings from the hatchway, immediately came forward and shouted down at the furious Dumas, "The ring first, you crook. The ring."

Dumas stopped in his tracks, wondering if this clever move by Sam was their way to ensure compliance with the agreement. Recognising that his only course was to bluff his way, he bowed gracefully and replied, "Of course, of course. Why, brother, what brings you to England?"

"In truth, I was chasing a fair maid," Jean replied.

At this, Dumas started to laugh. "You, chasing a woman?" Totally bemused by his brother's admission of a romance,

Dumas began walking up the gangplank. And as if to show he was an honest broker, he produced the ring from a pocket inside his tunic.

Jean held out a glass. "Shall we seal the deal with wine?"

Richard, meanwhile, had retrieved the bag of gold and, as if to be playing fair, held it out. "Shall we exchange then? Or do you wish to see the maiden your brother is chasing? She is below."

While this was all taking place, Sam had not been idle. He had run down the dock then back up the side streets to come down the harbour to the stanchion at the bow of the boat. He was aware that if he untied the boat, which had never turned about since arriving, it would pivot on the stern rope – a move that many of the boats used to go to sea.

The men on board were now busy trying to manoeuvre Dumas into the cabin below and were teasing with him by holding out the gold, while he was trying to give over the ring – but not till he was sure he had the bag. This ungainly tango, with each trying to gain an advantage, continued for some minutes.

Suddenly, almost by a stroke of serendipity, the boat made a sudden lurch as Sam released the bow rope, and Richard – gambling on the outcome – dropped the bag down the hatchway. Dumas made his first error by diving for it, hoping to scoop it up and leap off the boat. Richard immediately seized his chance and pushed the 15 stone Frenchman down the hatchway stairs, so that he arrived in a heap at the bottom. The Magistrate had been hiding there, and he quickly disabled the sprawling Dumas, tying his arms and legs before he had a chance to fight back. The rogue let out wild noises like a bear being encaged, as he was unceremoniously dumped in the prepared cabin. The door was then quickly shut and locked.

Sam, who by now knew the importance of releasing the stern rope before the boat swung too far and crashed into the dock, had already reached the second stanchion to unhitch the rope and allow the *Fleur* to start her journey to France.

Richard immediately realised that the young lad had saved the day.

"Find Lady Ann and tell her everything," he shouted. "I am sure she will reward you for your services, and tell her I'll be back in a month, on the usual date. She will understand."

Dumas's burly henchmen had already wandered off, realising that all had been lost and that chasing the agile Sam would achieve nothing.

Chapter 9

# The Delivery

After all the days of planning, the party on board *La Petite Fleur* felt almost cheated that a young lad of 12 had, almost single-handedly, solved all their problems. However, they were thankful that in the end they had their man and both the gold and the ring, which Dumas had dropped as he crashed down the hatchway stairs.

What the party did not expect or appreciate was the storm which greeted them as they neared the French coast, and they were very thankful when they eventually tied up at Calais in the early hours.

While it would have been difficult to muster a suitable escort for Dumas if he was just a thief, his real name of Philippe Perevade had a certain notoriety. Furthermore, with a murder charge of a young girl and the production of the warrant, the authorities were easily persuaded to spare a few men to ensure his delivery to Saint Etienne, in southern France, for trial.

Dumas, or Philippe Perevade as the warrant spelled out, was shackled inside a jail cart which lumbered on at no more than five miles an hour. Allowing for stops and overnight stays, it would take at least 15 days to arrive at its destination, probably more.

Richard, after ensuring the prisoner was indeed secure, and having made sure the three men who were charged with his delivery would not succumb to a bribe, as well as being strong enough to overpower a belligerent Dumas, decided to go ahead on horseback alone. He had business he needed to attend to in Paris.

Jean Perevade, although wanting to be at the trial, also decided to make his own way there. It would be at least a month before any trial date was set, giving him plenty of time to attend to a few of his own affairs on the way.

Lawrence Courtney, meanwhile, was now satisfied his task was done and he returned to Newhaven on *La Petite Fleur*, having been handsomely rewarded by Richard for all his troubles over the last few days and weeks.

Back at the Pilgrim, things were getting back to normal. Locals who had been avoiding the Pilgrim because the over-generous Dumas was becoming a bit tedious and most did not want to feel they were in debt to such a man, now resumed their routine of a lunchtime pint.

A day after the capture, Sam was about his usual chores and had been told to clear out Dumas's old room and set a new fire, ready for any new guest. He was shovelling the ash from the grate when he noticed a discarded note which had been tightly folded and scrunched up, and presumably meant to be burned.

Sam read it slowly. "*G, si pas de retour par cinq heures liberez moi à Màcon.*"[8] While Sam could not speak French, he guessed the words *liberez moi* probably meant something like 'liberate me'. He put the paper in his pocket and quickly finished his task, then slipped out to find Lady Ann who he knew would be at the Red Post.

Ann was indeed there and saw young Sam walk up to the inn from her window. *Strange*, she said to herself. Realising

---

[8] G, if not returned by five o'clock free me at Macon.

something must be up, she tripped downstairs to find Sam, who beamed when he saw her.

"Well, Sam, do you have some news for me?"

"Just this," he said, and handed her the note.

"Where and when did you find this?"

"In Dumas's room just this morning when I was clearing out the grate for a new customer."

"Well, if this was written by him, it seems he may have put a plan into action if he did not come back from the boat, which of course he didn't. And that in no small measure was due to your efforts." Ann ruffled the boy's hair in a friendly way as she said this. "I had better warn my husband, but Macon is in southern France on the way to Lyon."

"Well, *La Petite Fleur* is due back this evening," said Sam.

"That boat is becoming almost a second home," she said, and a smile spread across her face.

"Sam, my lad, can you do me a favour and have the blacksmith's trap here by 4pm, so I can be at the harbour ready to hire the boat for a trip across the Channel? Here, this should cover the hire charge and leave a bit for your troubles." Ann tipped several coins into the lad's hand and sent him on his way.

Knowing she would have to travel quickly if she was to catch up, or at least get a message to prevent Dumas's escape, Ann packed only a small bag then went downstairs to pay the innkeeper for her room and a little extra to cover storage for the items she was leaving behind.

At 4pm, as requested, Sam arrived with the trap, and the two set off back to the harbour. As the tide came in, so did *La Petite Fleur*. Once the boat was tied up, Ann went aboard to persuade the captain to sail back across the Channel as soon as the tide would allow. As she stepped aboard, who should she meet exiting from a cabin but Lawrence Courtney, the ex-Magistrate who had been partly instrumental in Dumas's capture.

When Ann showed him the note, he realised that urgent action was required to ensure all the weeks of spying on their prey and previous preparations were not thwarted.

"I'll be back at five," he told her. "First there are a few things I must attend to, but I will be happy to accompany you to Macon to ensure our prisoner does not escape." Then he went to the captain and suggested he took the boat to the south steps; that would ensure they would not need to wait for high tide.

Thus, a few hours later *La Petit Fleur* set sail again for Calais, with Ann Carlton and Lawrence Courtney aboard. The ex-Magistrate had had the forethought to seek out some maps of France, and the couple pored over them to see the likely route the jail cart might take, and how they might catch up with it.

"If we can only get to it before it reaches Macon, we may be able to suggest a diversion and leave Dumas's cronies in the lurch," said Lawrence. "After all, we do not know how many 'friends' may be in the ambush party, and if we can avoid a confrontation so much the better.

"If we can get the posse to take the old road to the east of the Loire, after say reaching Tournus, they can bypass Macon and rejoin the Lyon Road at Beauregard," he added.

"Yes, there are some steep hills down to Macon on the main road where an ambush could easily be mounted, while the eastern path is not so hilly," said Ann, who knew the area from her many travels to Lyon.

They discussed other possible detours, but in the end they agreed the eastern path would be the most likely to succeed in avoiding any ambush. The only problem was that no doubt Dumas would have spies out to track the path of the jail cart, so they needed to spring their detour at the last minute to ensure the 'escape party' would not have time to make alternative plans and ambush elsewhere.

"I wonder if there is a spare jail cart at perhaps Dijon, or with luck another captive on his way south that would mislead our would-be escapee," mused Ann.

"That would be one way of misleading them, but somehow, I doubt it would work. Indeed, we may have difficulty in persuading the officials minding Dumas to change route anyway, and lose track of which cart is ours," replied Lawrence.

Ann agreed. "Now, as we will be riding long hours to catch them up – after all, they will have nearly two days' lead – I think some sleep is in order."

"You're quite right," said Lawrence.

So they quietly ate some bread and pate Ann had brought with her, then each retired to get some rest before their exertions of the next day.

## Chapter 10

# The Chase

The crossing this time was not too rough, and the boat made good progress, arriving at Calais in the early hours. On arriving at port, the party wasted no time in hiring horses and were about to set off on the road to Saint Quentin when Lawrence thought he better check that their man was indeed ahead of them. Unfortunately, so early in the day, almost no-one was about. The port authorities did not have knowledge of which road the jail cart had taken, just that it had left two days ago. They then called at the local jailhouse, but no-one was in attendance.

"Everybody seems to have had a good time last night," said Lawrence jokingly.

They were pondering on whether just to ride towards Arras, when Ann suggested they at least get some breakfast, and perhaps someone at the inn down the street may help. Tying up their horses outside, they entered the inn to find the innkeeper's wife was up even though it was only 4:30am.

"Bon matin," she said.

Ann, who of course who spoke fluent French, asked for 'croissant et café' and then asked if the woman had any news of a jail cart passing two days before. Alas, she did not. She told Ann that she was often quite busy early in the morning, so it might have passed by without her seeing anything.

Over their croissants and coffee, they pondered what they should do next.

"I think we should ride to Arras," said Lawrence. "That way we will get some distance under our belts. It may be quite late when we get there, but hopefully we can find people who will know about our fugitive."

Ann agreed, so the party paid for their vitals, remounted their horses, and headed off down the well-trodden road to Arras. They rode at a good pace, stopping only briefly at Bruay-la-Buissiere to have some refreshment and to change horses, and reached Arras very late in the evening.

They rode straight to the Gendarmerie Office to enquire about their fugitive.

Ann was tasked with interrogating the clerk, who seemed somewhat surprised that anybody should want to know about a common criminal in a jail cart. Yes, he had passed that way about a day-and-a-half ago, the man confirmed, but he was not aware of the party's destination or route.

Ann persisted. "Do you not keep records of who passes?"

"Not unless they actually stop here for the night," answered the clerk.

"I think we had better press on to Saint Quentin," said Ann. "I hope they are not going via Paris. The irony is that Richard has almost certainly gone to Paris on State business, but he will not of course be concerned about the passage of our quarry."

"Fine, but not tonight," said Lawrence, so they found an inn where they could get a meal and a bed for the night.

Although they again rose early the next morning, it was still late in the evening when they rode into Saint Quentin on their fourth change of horses.

Ann was becoming a little frustrated as the capture of Dumas should have meant they could control their expenditure, but now they were shelling out so much on horses and accommodation that she wondered if it had been worthwhile.

Once again at St Quentin, they were obstructed by lack of officials being accessible, so headed to an inn to see if they could glean any news. The innkeeper had no knowledge of any jail cart coming through for months, but when the name of Philippe Perevade was mentioned, to Lawrence's surprise the man asked, "Was he not the man they were looking for in connection with a murder down south at Saint Etienne?"

"Oui," said Lawrence, whose ears pricked up when the town was mentioned. The innkeeper explained he had read about the case in the newspapers and, realising the two visitors had some genuine interest in the subject, he asked some of the other customers in the bar if they had any news. None seemed to think any jail cart had passed recently, but most were from out of town, so their information was of little consequence.

Ann and Lawrence were feeling a little despondent and decided that to seek rooms and rest, so they could be fresh for the chase in the morning.

When the two met the next morning, Ann was a little brighter in mood. "I have just remembered that Richard has an acquaintance in Reims, a certain Christian Du Pont who may be able to help us. If he sends a message to Richard in Paris, at least we can, in effect, cover both roads south. "

They wasted no time eating their breakfast, and by a few minutes past eight they were heading off down the road.

Although by midday the spires of Reims Cathedral were seen in the distance, it was many hours later that they turned into the Boulevard Louis Roederer, rode up to a rather grand house, and knocked on the door.

The door was opened by a servant, and Ann explained who they were. After a few moments, they were ushered inside.

"Bienvenue, bienvenue," said a smiling, jovial man, with a clean-shaven round face. "Pourquoi, combien d'années est-ce?[9]"

Ann, for the benefit of Lawrence, replied in English. "I think it was four years back in Paris. Have you had any recent news from my husband? Only, he is almost certainly in Paris, and I need to get a message to him, but we are in a dilemma chasing a fugitive." Ann then explained him the whole story, although initially she left out the fact that the murdered girl had been her sister.

Christian Du Pont felt there was more to the story as Ann seemed to have been both sides of the Channel chasing her prey, and eventually, with tears welling up in her eyes, she admitted the girl was her sister Teresa.

"Mon Dieu!" exclaimed Christian, and he immediately ensured one of his trusted servants was dispatched to Paris with a message for Richard Carlton.

Ann visibly relaxed now that she was sure her husband would soon know the situation. His position as Ambassador would ensure any fugitive passing on any route to Saint Etienne would be carefully monitored. Indeed, they decided to accept Christian's offer of dinner and a bed for the night.

The next morning, after a hearty breakfast, they left on their journey south. But despite having travelled at a break-neck speed these last few days, they made it only to Chalons en Champagne before again resting at a suitable hostelry.

Their next destination of Troyes was mostly over reasonable ground, and they made good time, even though it was nightfall before they arrived. As they had not come across Dumas, and there was no news of an escorted prisoner along that road, they decided the jail cart must have taken the prisoner via Paris. However, they

---

[9] Why, how many years is it?

still did not know if they would reach Macon first. The two paths would not meet until they reached Beaune, which was 35 kilometres south of Dijon, and that was a further 190 kms.

That night, as they relaxed in front of an open fire Lawrence decided perhaps there was a way of at least confirming where the escort was if they took a lesser road southwest to Auxerre. This town lay on the route from Paris to Beaune. That way they would still have time to intercept before Dumas got near Macon. They estimated their speedier passage must put them roughly level latitude-wise. This allowed for the two days lead the cart carrying Dumas had and the initial road to Paris being longer and the jail cart moving slower than them.

With fresh horses, they set off next morning towards Auxerre, and by mid-afternoon were crossing the Serein River. As they were moving along past the Abbey Church at Pontigny, from a side road came a large black dog that barked and snapped at the heels of Ann's horse. Before she could calm her steed, it reared up and deposited her on the hard road. In trying to rise, she realised that she had badly sprained her left ankle in the fall. The dog that had caused the commotion disappeared as quickly as it arrived, but it was clear they could travel no further that day, and not until Ann could at least put some weight on her foot. Lawrence helped her into the saddle, and they made their way slowly to the Moulin de Pontigny, which was run as a boarding house for travellers.

Lawrence eased Ann from her mount and assisted her into the building and up only a short flight of stairs. By now he had sufficient French to obtain 'deux chambres', being adjoining rooms with a view over the river. He then ordered 'déjeuner' for them both.

That evening, Ann sat with her foot immersed in cold then warm water, and after dinner taken in her room, they both retired for the night.

In the morning, although her ankle showed signs of improvement, she would need at least another day's rest to ensure no lasting damage.

Lawrence reviewed the map. "If I ride on my own with a good horse, I should be in Auxerre in less than five hours. I can then hopefully get news of our quarry and return here by nightfall."

So, leaving Ann to rest, Lawrence raced off to Auxerre. It was about 1pm when he arrived and went straight to the office of the local Gendarmerie to enquire if Dumas had passed. Regrettably, there was no news, and Lawrence was about to leave when a stout gentleman, who was himself an officer of the Gendarmerie, tapped him on the shoulder.

"Do you look for a man named Philip Perevade?" the man asked in English but with a southern French accent.

"Oui, oui," said Lawrence, somewhat surprised by this question.

"Well, I delivered him to Paris where he was to be held for at least three or four days until his transport could be arranged to Saint Etienne for trial."

"So, he will not have left Paris yet then?" said Lawrence with a sigh.

"Well, not until tomorrow at the earliest."

"This is good news indeed, for there could be a plot to ambush the posse and release him near Macon."

"How do you know that?" asked the Frenchman.

Lawrence then took the man aside and explained the whole story.

"Well, I can ensure the posse are made aware of this."

"It may not be as simple as that," said Lawrence. "We expect Dumas will have his spies who will probably be monitoring his progress, and it is difficult to know how many men he can muster. I have been studying the map and think it would be best if the jail cart went to the east of the Saône , after say Tournus, bypassing Macon and rejoining the usual road at Beauregarde. That way, hopefully, he will be safely delivered to Saint Etienne before his 'amis' realise they have been tricked."

"I think that is a good idea, and I can also see that it is better that the posse know little of this until the last minute, to avoid careless talk that could be overheard, or perhaps bribed from them," said the Frenchman. "I will have a word with my superiors and see if I can rejoin the posse when they reach here. That way I can make the move to the alternative road at the last moment."

Lawrence felt that at last their quarry would not be sprung, and he shook the man warmly by the hand. "Quel est votre nom?"

"Je m'appelle Andre Merle," he replied.

"Très bien," said Lawrence with a laugh.

He then explained that he must return to Pontigny straight away, as he needed to give the news to Lady Ann. As Andre was puzzled as to who Ann was, Lawrence found himself explaining the situation and that she was the sister of the girl who had been murdered by the infamous Dumas, who was now being taken for trial for her murder.

On hearing this, Andre said he would personally deliver the rogue to the doors of the jail in St Etienne.

It was quite late when Lawrence finally returned to Moulin de Pontigny with the good news. Now they could proceed at an orderly pace to St Etienne without the burden of how to muster extra men to prevent Dumas's escape.

# Chapter 11

# The Changeling

Although Dumas was initially furious that he had been captured and was now penned in the wretched jail cart, he was still as cunning as ever. He felt he was still in control by ensuring an escape plan had been in place before the fateful day when he had found himself forced to board the boat by the actions of a mere 12-year-old. He knew he could rely on his old friends at Macon to release him, so set about getting his posse to be as relaxed as possible and easier to catch off guard.

This meant Dumas decided to be very cooperative on the road to Paris, and he proved himself to be a model prisoner, obeying every instruction and making no attempt to escape. Even when he was incarcerated in the large jail in Paris for nearly a week, he never once complained about his conditions. Indeed, his polite and disciplined demeanour effectively fooled the authorities so much that he was sent on his way to Saint Etienne in a mere stagecoach, rather than a jail cart. This was easier for everyone, as they could make better time, and the well-sprung stagecoach meant Dumas could snooze and think out a plan to fool any witnesses, should his release plan fail and he be forced to stand trial.

Dumas, or Philippe Perevade, was realising that his only defence would be the same ploy he had used before – pretending to be his brother. So, he quietly imitated his brother whenever the occasion allowed. Any conversation he had was now using phrases and mannerisms of his brother, which he had previously perfected a few years ago when charged with theft. To complete the change to his mother's first born, he would need to lose a little weight by only eating sufficient to keep his body working and doing some modest exercise in the coach from time to time.

Although one of his guards was seated opposite him, the posse took turns on occupying the coach and invariably used this time to take a nap. They were becoming quite blasé, lulled into a false sense that this person was of some repute and rather than thinking of Dumas as a prisoner, viewed him as someone special who they were accompanying to a chosen destination. Indeed, they knew little of the terrible crimes Dumas had been responsible for, and they began to echo the courtesies he showed to them, chatting politely on all manner of subjects. Dumas even moved the subject of their conversation to engineering, to see if he could hold his own without being caught out, as he knew his brother had knowledge of such matters.

When Dumas got to Auxerre, his posse changed, so he had to re-establish his compliant, friendly persona. He was pleased to note that within a day he had again relaxed his party so much that the man inside with him would be chatting and joking as if they were old friends, rather than prisoner and jailer. This pattern continued through the following days, with Dumas acting like a trusted servant.

At Beaune, Andre Merle – the gendarme who had been warned of an escape attempt by Lawrence – was now part of the posse, and he was able to send a message to Ann and Lawrence. He advised that Dumas was being very cooperative, but nevertheless Andre was preparing to change the route after Tournus, as planned. He had not yet spied anybody noting their progress, but would not expect this until they reached, or shortly after leaving Tournus.

## La Nuit à Therouanne

Andre then returned to his task of jailer. After Beaune, they journeyed on to Chalon-sur-Saône and then on to Tournus, where Andre ensured they had fresh horses. He even spent an extra day at this stop, hoping he might spy anyone who could be one of Dumas's men. He felt that if there was indeed an escape plan brewing, Dumas would have one of his cronies watching when they left Tournus to ensure they did not cross the Saone there and go via Cuisery. Andre was playing a waiting game as much as Dumas, who was still relaxed and not wanting to upset his jailers. He wore neither leg irons nor was he shackled to the coach, which Andre was aware was a risk. But he had not informed his fellow gendarmes of his plan, or even that there may be an ambush to release their prisoner.

Before they got to Tournus, they took supper at a convenient inn about three kilometres out. Andre made sure the prisoner was well fed and even ensured he was not spared for want of ale. Dumas was not worried or suspicious of this bounty; after all, it would be nearly a day-and-a-half before they got to Macon, so there was plenty of time to sober up and be prepared.

About a kilometre before reaching the town of Tournus, a rider came up quite close to the coach, then passed by slowly. Andre noticed how the man was carefully looking to see who might be inside, and as soon as he was apparently happy that the coach did indeed contain Dumas, the rider quickened his pace and rode off ahead. The coach maintained its same pace, but just when the posse were thinking they were now on the direct road to Macon, Andre said he would take the reins of the coach and let his fellow gendarme ride alongside.

During this changeover he quietly told his compatriot his plan, ensuring that he did not speak a word of it to his friend sitting inside the coach.

Although not such a good road, there was just one more bridge across the Saône, about 15km out from Tournus. Thus, turning off the direct road to Macon, Andre had the coach across the river and onto this lesser-known road without the party inside the coach even noticing the slight change in direction. The weather helped, as it was a dark, drizzly day, so there was no sun to give away the brief change in direction onto the new route.

By nightfall they had reached Arbigny on the east side of the Saône. Andre now ensured that both his fellow gendarmes were aware of complete secrecy as to where they were and the route they would now take. The next morning, when they journeyed south with the sun now appearing from the correct direction, Dumas was still relaxed. In a few hours he expected to be disappearing into the vast vineyards that surrounded them.

Two hours went by, and Dumas bravely asked, "How far to Macon?"

"Why, about 12 kilometres," was the answer.

Dumas sat back and waited for the noise of riders on the road behind, but none came. Not wanting to give the game away he tried to spy familiar landmarks that would give him a clue as to where they were. But after two hours in desperation, he asked again, "How long until we get to Macon?"

"We decided to press on and not call at Macon."

This answer totally confused Dumas. How could they miss out Macon, when they had to pass through it to get to Lyon. So, he asked again. "Surely we must come to Macon soon?"

"Not on the east bank of the Saône. Our next stop is just up ahead at Pont-de-Veyle."

"East bank! When did we cross the Saône?" Dumas was shocked.

"Why yesterday, on the road to Arbigny."

"I've been duped, completely wrong-footed," Dumas muttered to himself, furious that he had not noticed. Then he remembered the heavy meal he'd enjoyed just short of Tournus. *How stupid he had been.*

He was about to rage at his captors for their trickery when he remembered that his only defence now was to play the good guy, and he sat back in his seat, completely deflated. He realised, as did Andre Merle, that even if his friends realised something was wrong and that the coach must have taken another route, gathering the ambush group together to set up an escape plan elsewhere would be almost impossible.

The rest of the journey passed without incident, and thus a week later – having travelled through Lyon, where Dumas spent two nights – he was eventually delivered to the jail in Saint Etienne.

A day later he was brought before an examining judge (juge d'instruction) who questioned the public prosecutor (le procureur) at some length. Once the charges had been read and the details established that this Philippe Perevade was the last person seen near the poor victim, Teresa, the judge ordered the matter to go to trial. In view of one of the charges being murder, bail was refused – not that Dumas even asked for it. A date was then set for the trial two weeks hence, to start on July 14$^{th}$ – just two days short of two years since the dreadful rape and murder had taken place.

Dumas still had some credit with a rather shady gentleman who found him a defence counsellor, Olivier Le Genaux. A tall man with a droopy moustache, he was known as an expert for getting people off, even when there had been overwhelming evidence against them.

Oliver Le Genaux asked to be able to question his client, and Dumas was taken out of his cell into a small room within the jail.

Behind the locked door, the counsellor questioned Dumas for some time about the charges. Dumas answered as if he had read the details in a newspaper, deliberately keeping the terrible deeds at arm's length.

This was deliberate, as he knew they could not provide a lot of evidence that he had even been at the inn when Teresa was murdered. He only remembered meeting briefly with the innkeeper before going up to Teresa's room. Dumas knew well enough that he must keep any incriminating details to himself, so he made no mention of visiting the inn, of how Teresa had been all smiles and flirting outrageously with him and then, when Dumas started to take things further, she had pushed him back. Dumas was not one to be turned down, and this had enraged him so much that the rape and murder followed in a matter of minutes.

Oliver Le Genaux was, of course, in the dark, unaware of these thoughts going through Dumas's mind. He considered what evidence there was to place his client at the scene, and felt at this stage there was not much to even identify the culprit. Then when Philippe Perevade advised that his brother Jean was an identical twin and would almost certainly be at the trial, a smile came over the counsellor's face.

"I am sure I can bring enough doubt in the jury's mind to have you free before the month is out," he said. "However," said Oliver, "if you were not there at the scene of the murder, you will need to have been elsewhere!"

"Well, I was at the wedding of a niece," replied Dumas.

Whether this was true or not was of no matter at this stage; Oliver just needed a witness to say Dumas was elsewhere on the day of the murder.

His client was again economical with the truth, venturing few details of the wedding. In practice, he had indeed gone to the wedding after he had raped Teresa. But he doubted there would be much mention of timing, and as the incident had been two years ago, even 30 minutes here or there would be of no consequence.

"What is the name of your niece? Can we call her as a witness?" asked Oliver.

"I should think so, but she will have to be tutored, if you see my meaning, as she can never remember anything. I doubt she even remembers her own birthday. She only got married to her husband because her father wanted her off his hands and paid a sum that the poor fool could not refuse!' Dumas explained. "Her name is Gisèle Dèrnier. I suggest you don't call anybody else from the family, but I expect her husband will be pleased to have her out of his hair for a day or two, by being here in Saint Etienne. They live southwest of here, at Le Puy."

Oliver said he would get one of his clerks to make arrangement to have the woman there, ready for the trial. He also said he doubted he needed to ask any more questions, so he was unlikely to see Dumas again until the day before the trial, when he would know what witnesses, if any, were being called.

"Alors, there is one thing further," said Dumas. "An English gentleman called Richard Carlton may appear and is likely to take an interest in the case. I believe he may think I stole something from him, but strangely, if you ask him directly, he is likely to dismiss it of no consequence. Shall we just say, mention of such matters of theft will 'muddy the waters', but if you find you need to get rid of this aspect, be bold and ask him directly. He will almost certainly say something like 'it's a private matter' and not proceed further."

"Well," said Oliver. "Is there any truth in it?"

"There may have been, but the property has been returned. Shall we just say it was a pure misunderstanding."

Peter Gatenby

    Oliver looked a little puzzled but decided that as the charges were murder and rape, a theft was a minor point. So, he left his client to while away the next two weeks in a rather stuffy, airless cell, being high summer at Saint Etienne.

# Chapter 12

# Serendipity

The day of the trial approached, and all the parties with an interest made their arrangements to be there. While it would be the State Prosecutor making the case for the prosecution, Ann felt she should be defending her sister from this evil man. She still felt it was ironic that a man who looked the same could also be such a kind and thoughtful person. But while the name Philippe made her shudder, when Jean came to the hotel where she was staying and courteously re-introduced himself, she relaxed and beamed at him.

"May I get you something to drink?" he asked.

"Merci, oui, un café s'il te plaît," she said.

Jean was temporarily stunned by her request – not the nature of it; a coffee was easy to come by. But the word 'te' or 'tu' was only used within members of a family or very close friends.

So, when he returned with two coffees, he was quick to say how pleased he was to meet her again and then apologised because it was a member of his family that meant she would now face the ordeal of the trial the next day.

Rather than become despondent, Ann sat upright and took Jean's hand. "I feel it is wise for me to get to know you very well," she said. "I do not want to be pointing at the wrong person if I am asked to identify him. You have mentioned before how he confused juries into believing he was you. On those occasions you were not about to defend your good name or malign his.

This time the jury will be confounded if the judge asks you to stand next to the prisoner so a choice can be made.

"Obviously, I can ask you for a password, and even here I can see the brooch tucked neatly under your lapel. This would be more than enough for me to tell you apart, but the jury may not cotton onto the significance of such facts. I have, however, one thing that has struck me that will definitively tell you two apart, but I cannot be sure until I see your brother. That said, I have never actually been in his presence, but of course Richard has, and he described you as *'deux petits pois dela même pod'*." With that, they both chuckled.

Jean supped his coffee and replied, "If indeed you have some special way of telling us apart, you would be better than my mother. With my brother forever tricking me into doing wrong or persuading my mother or father that I had been up to some mischief of his doing, she was inclined to think we were as bad as each other and often called us by the wrong names. The only saving grace is that it was me who came to her aid when she became terminally ill, so the last few weeks of her life she knew what a dutiful son could be. Just occasionally she would look into my eyes and say, 'Is that you, Philippe?' But I forgave her, as she would kiss my hand when I did her a kindness, or returned in a hurry from some business or other. My father died when I – or should I say we – was only twelve, and in Philippe's case that was when his minor pranks turned into deliberate acts of thuggery and thieving."

At this point, Lawrence Courtney appeared. "Mon Dieu," said Jean. "I thought you were back en Angleterre?"

"Ah well, Ann may not have told you, but your brother left a message back at the Pilgrim for his compatriots to release him near Macon, if we managed to capture him. It seems your brother is always one step ahead of us. We only knew because

## La Nuit à Therouanne

eagle-eyed Sam came across a note that should have been burned. Fortunately, with the aid of a gendarme called Andre Merle, we were able to ensure the posse went across to the east side of the Saône and bypass Macon. I have just been up to the jail to check things out. Apparently, he has hired a certain Oliver Le Genaux, who has a reputation for getting people off despite being known to have committed terrible crimes."

"It seems Ann is right to be able to tell me from him then. For your benefit, we have previously used a password 'there are no roses today', although as long as you say something about roses, we will realise who is who. Furthermore, you will note if I finger my lapel here that I have the small brooch which Lady Ann gave me some months ago. It was a test, since my brother stole an identical one at the time of the murder of her poor sister. The very fact that I was willing to wear it proved to Ann that I could not be my brother."

"Ingenious. I get the feeling your brother is a bit of a chameleon. Presumably, as far as we know, your brother does not still have this brooch to confound us?"

"No, he would have been searched many times since he left Calais, and knowing my brother he probably pawned it straight away to gain funds to escape to Angleterre."

Ann suggested they take a stroll through the town to a small café near *Le Jardin des Plantes* where they could get lunch. "We had better get some exercise, mon amis, as we could spend many days just sitting in court."

So, the party rose and wandered down the streets and through a market. Ann was looking about for pawnbrokers' shops. She did not say anything, but Jean's remark about his brother Philippe pawning the other brooch had left her wondering. By now it would almost certainly be displayed for sale; after all, Dumas would not have had the opportunity, or want to redeem the item. So, she tarried a little each time they went past a jeweller or pawnbroker. She made the excuse that she was looking for a gift for her husband who had a birthday in a week, rather than come straight out with the fact that she was looking for the brooch.

They were nearing the café when a silver watch caught her eye, and then to her amazement she thought she spotted the brooch just behind it.

"You go on, gentlemen. The Café du Fleurs de Soleil is just around the corner. I will see you there." And with that she disappeared into the shop.

"Bonjour, madame, vous êtes venu racheter un article?"[10].

"Non, non. S'il vous plais, je veux acheter l'horloge pour mon mari."[11]

The shopkeeper leaned into the shop window display, and in order to retrieve the gentleman's pocket watch, he brought out the brooch as well and placed them both on the counter. Ann immediately turned it over and saw that not only did it match the missing brooch, but there was the small 'T' for Teresa inscribed on the back.

"Je vais prendre les deux."

"Les deux, madame?"

"Oui."

With that the shopkeeper smiled. He had not expected her to purchase both, but as business was very slow, he did not hesitate to start wrapping the two items.

"Combien, monsieur?"

"Vingt-cinq francs."

---

[10] You come to redeem an article.
[11] No, no. If you, please I wish to buy the watch for my husband.

## La Nuit à Therouanne

Having found a box and wrapped the gentleman's pocket watch, he was about to wrap the brooch as well, when Ann took it off the counter and said she would wear it immediately.

Gazing at the brooch, she said, "Une si jolie pièce, qui l'a apportée, peut-être une dame qui tombe dans les moments difficiles?"[12]

"Non, madame. Alors Monsieur Phillipe Perevade, voila." Placing his book of deposits on the counter, the man pointed out the entry. "Aussi le nom sur le billet."

"Quel surprise," said Ann, pretending that she had expected it to be from a lady. She asked to keep the now redundant ticket, and the shopkeeper obligingly agreed – after all, it would just have been thrown away.

Having paid, Ann left the shop. Her two companions had gone ahead as she had requested, so she took the brooch and carefully pinned it, with its ticket, inside her bodice where it could not be seen. 'I have you now, Monsieur Philippe,' she said to herself.

A few moments later she turned into a sunny corner where the café was situated and found that the two men had already obtained a table with a view of the garden, which had an impressive show of sunflowers and lupins.

"Were you successful?" asked Jean.

"Oh, very successful," replied Ann, but she only showed them the pocket watch, which both agreed was very desirable and an excellent choice as a gift.

"Will your husband be at the trial?" asked Lawrence.

"Why of course. But he sent word that he will not be here until tomorrow. He may just miss the preliminaries, but knows

---

[12] Such a pretty piece, who brought it in, perhaps a lady falling on hard time?

he may be called, as he of course held the warrant and carried out the arrest."

The party lingered over le déjeuner, consuming a little more alcohol than perhaps they should, but in the warm sunshine they made the most of this brief period when they could relax... "pour demain est un autre jour".

At about 3:30pm, Ann said she needed to see 'le procureur' as she was to be called as a witness, and she wanted to ensure they both had all the details correct. The fact that she now had extra incriminating evidence was not mentioned.

Jean immediately rose and said, "I will accompany you."

However, Ann felt that at this stage appearing in front of 'le procureur' would confuse him, so she gently declined the offer.

"No, that is quite okay. I have already arranged for a coach from the hotel to be here about now. It will take me there and return me to the hotel about 5:30pm."

Seeing that Jean looked a little peeved that his genuine concern had been rebuffed, she added, "However, you can escort me to dinner this evening. But do not worry about carrying a rose. I think I can recognise you by now."

With that the party laughed.

A few minutes later the coach arrived, and Ann was soon on her way.

The two gentlemen paid the café bill and wandered off, taking a different longer route back to the hotel. When they passed a florist, Jean said with a twinkle in his eye, "Come, we will buy some roses." And he ushered his friend into the shop.

"Bonjour, madame, deux roses, s'il vous plait, mais convient aux boutonnières pour nos revers."[13]

---

[13] Good day madam two roses please but suitable for buttonholes for our lapels.

Thus, when the two gentlemen appeared to escort Ann in for dinner that evening with white roses in their buttonholes, she smiled and laughed. "It is lucky Richard is not about, otherwise he may just think I have fallen for you, Jean. Is this our wedding breakfast, and Lawrence the best man?"

The party dissolved into peals of laughter but, realising they were 'making a scene', went into dine.

*Chapter 13*

# Too much information can spoil the game
### *(Trop d'informations peuvent ruiner le jeu)*

The day of the trial dawned. Dumas was confident he could pull his doppelganger trick again. After all, this time he did not need witnesses that he was elsewhere, except perhaps the hapless Gisèle. He was confident that Oliver Le Genaux could easily persuade the court to look about and see other men who would fit his description, and hey presto, there would be Jean looking so alike that it would be as if someone had put a big mirror in the gallery to reflect himself. A menacing smile came over his face as he imagined the gasp from the jury when they spotted the 'other Dumas'.

*This is going to be fun*, he thought. In this good mood, he could maintain his composure and act as an honest and thoughtful man, just like his brother.

He was escorted to the court, handcuffed to a gendarme, at 8:30am. It was only a five-minute walk, but they needed to have him locked into the small, raised box at the side of the court for the trial to begin at 9am sharp.

The court filled up quickly with witnesses, the counsellors for prosecution and defence, as well as many locals, and reporters. This case had attracted a lot of publicity at the time of the murder, and when word had got round that the perpetrator was now in the local jail, the date for the trial had been marked in everybody's diary. All the hotels and inns were doing brisk business, and by the time this day arrived there was hardly a room left unfilled.

At nine o'clock, the judge Michel Regarde entered and took his seat. The public gallery was full with reporters, as well as Jean, Lawrence, and Ann, who had arrived very early to ensure they had a seat. It was unlikely that Ann would be called until the next day, and she had a special reason for wanting to be sitting behind the accused.

The clerk of the court read the charges, and the prosecution briefly laid out their case. There was no doubt as to how Teresa had been murdered, nevertheless the prosecutor, Monsieur Pascal Canton, first called a Superintendent Gendarme appointed by 'le sous-préfet de l'arrondissement de Saint-Étienne' to deal with this crime – Gendarme Alain Lamas.

"Monsieur Lamas, please tell the court what you found when you attended at the Hotel Grande on the afternoon of 16th July, 1842."

"I found the body of a young girl who had been raped and murdered. Initially it had been difficult to tell how she had died, as the body had been slashed as if to mark it, like a criminal might mark some item he had stolen to say, 'mine, do not touch'. It was a terrible scene, and one which I hope I never see again."

The prosecutor continued, "Did you find any evidence of who the perpetrator might have been?"

"It did appear that the girl in her dying moments had written something in her own blood upon the floor, which appeared to be 'oreiller'.[14] Later it was determined that she had been asphyxiated by a hand thrust against her throat, so we dismissed this 'pillow' as being of no consequence, although it did puzzle

---

[14] Pillow

me. Why she had written this was therefore a mystery, and I have been unable to find any connection with 'pillow' or any person."

"In that case, how did you come to identify the accused?"

"From interviewing the hotel owner, who was on duty at the time of the murder."

Having given his evidence, the gendarme was about to stand down when Oliver Le Genaux stood up.

"Your witness," said the judge, acknowledging his right to cross-examine.

The gendarme remained where he was, but the question he was asked was not one he was expecting.

"Monsieur, as well as the hotel owner, is there anybody else who saw the body, or who visited the victim that night?"

"Only the girl's sister," replied the gendarme. "It was she who discovered the body, but we gained little from her at the time, as the shock temporarily affected her so much that she was all but struck dumb."

"So, you have relied on just one witness that Monsieur Perevade was the possible perpetrator of this crime?"

"Well, yes, and the fact that his name was in the innkeeper's register as having stayed there at the time."

"You say at the time, monsieur. Can you be precise: was he booked in to stay there the night of 16th July?"

"Well, no, but he had stayed there the previous two nights, and other guests said they had seen Monsieur Perevade in the company of the girl Teresa Montelimar."

"But not booked in on the night of the 16th of July?"

"Non."

"Thank you." Turning towards the judge, Oliver said, "That is all I wish to say to this witness," then he sat down, satisfied he had sown a few seeds of doubt.

The prosecutor Pascal Canton then informed the judge he wished to call Monsieur Daniel Désir the proprietor of the Hotel Grande, who was thus brought into the court and sworn in.

"Monsieur Désir, you are the proprietor of the Hotel Grande?"

"Oui, monsieur."

"Were you on duty on the afternoon of 16th July, 1842?"

"Oui."

"Can you describe the circumstances in which you saw the accused?"

"It was about 2pm in the afternoon when Monsieur Perevade entered the hotel and asked which room Teresa Montelimar was residing in. I advised him, and he walked towards the stairs."

"What happened then?"

"It must have been about 20 minutes later that I heard a scream from upstairs. I was in the dining room at the time, but on going into the foyer, I found the lady's sister Ann in some distress. She could hardly speak, but just pointed in the direction of Teresa Montelimar's room. I went upstairs to find the terrible scene and immediately called for the Gendarmerie to attend."

"Did you see the accused again at the time, following his speaking to you earlier?"

"No, there was no sign of him!"

"Have you seen Monsieur Perevade since that day until now?"

"No."

Pascal Canton then looked to Oliver Le Genaux. "Your witness."

Oliver rose slowly. This was his moment when he knew he could throw the jury into confusion.

"Monsieur Désir, how long have you been the proprietor of Le Hotel Grande?"

"This will be the twentieth year."

"Did you give a description of Monsieur Perevade to the gendarme who attended?"

"Yes, I did."

"Please can you advise the court what that was?"

"I said they would be looking for a man in his early forties, about 1.8 metres tall, moderately built, with light auburn hair, dark eyes, and a beard."

"Why, that description would fit many men in this courtroom! Look about you, monsieur. Can you not see two or three people who would fit that description? Are you sure the person sitting behind the bar is the same man you saw going up the stairs all that time ago. Could other men of a different description not have gone up the same stairs while you were in the dining room?"

"I suppose so, but I recognised Monsieur Perevade because he had stayed with us."

"Well, look around, sir. Can you see anybody else that would fit your description?"

Daniel Désir looked about the court, at the jury, and then Oliver led his eye higher.

"How about the gentleman at the end in the gallery? Could he fit your description?"

As Daniel's eyes reached Jean, there was slight gasp – not just from him, but from the jury as well.

Judge Regard, now also puzzled by this gasp, looked up and saw Jean.

For a brief moment there was complete silence, then anybody who had not already compared the two was now doing so, and comments of *'Sacre Bleu'* and *'Formidable'* echoed around the court.

At this point the judge interceded. "Monsieur," he said to Jean. "What is your name?"

Jean remained calm. After all, he had been expecting this tactic. "Jean Perevade," he answered.

"Are you related to the accused?"

"He is my brother!"

"Monsieur, I would be grateful if you could come down into the court so that the jury can determine who is who."

Jean duly obliged. He knew Ann had yet to be called, but he was now confident she was able to see the difference. Indeed, he had heard her utter 'Yes' under her breath, as if she had finally seen some aspect of the face or bearing that could tell them apart. He remembered her talking in riddles about needing to be sure who was who, and that once she saw Philippe she would know. Quite what this key aspect was, he did not know – even their own mother had struggled at times. But he put his trust in her judgement and dutifully descended the stairs, entered the body of the court, and stood by the box that housed his brother.

Oliver Le Genaux now played the game which he had been rehearsing in his mind.

"Monsieur Désir, imagine it is the afternoon of 16$^{th}$ July, and a man comes into your hotel and asks to see Teresa Montelimar. Do you ask who he is?"

"I didn't need to. Monsieur Perevade had been with us the previous two nights."

"So, you do not know if it was this Monsieur Perevade, or this Monsieur Perevade?"

Then dramatically, he moved Jean to the other side of the box reserved for the accused.

"This Monsieur Perevade, or this Monsieur Perevade? Cet homme, ou cet homme?"

By now the poor hotel keeper was totally confused.

"But it was Philippe Perevade. His name was in the book," he replied in desperation.

## La Nuit à Therouanne

"Yes, but he did not stay there that night, and you never asked his name."

With that Oliver sat down, confident he had now almost defeated the prosecution's case.

The judge looked at the clock. "I think we will adjourn now for lunch," he said, and everyone rose as he left the court.

As soon as he had exited the courtroom, there was uproar. even the jury began chatting among themselves, questioning how they were meant to tell the men apart, and knowing they could hardly condemn both men.

Although Ann thought her husband would be called, as she went for lunch she was wondering if in practice this was now going to happen. His evidence was very procedural in how he had personally intervened to help arrest Count Dumas, as he was called in England; after all, there was no extradition treaty. However, the court seemed to think this was unnecessary, although of course they were indeed thankful for Richard Carlton for his help. They now saw it merely one of assistance through his office as an English Ambassador. In practice they knew little if anything about what Dumas had stolen, or indeed that Ann was his wife. There had been no need to record such details in the court papers.

Then an unexpected event took place. Oliver Le Genaux, the defence counsellor, came to the judge to plead with him to allow a defence witness to appear that afternoon, as her husband had been gravely injured in a riding accident and she would need to return to Le Puy as soon as possible. She may not be able to return for some days, or even weeks, leaving the trial and the key defence witness unheard.

In the ordinary course, the whole of the prosecution's case would be put first before any defence witnesses were heard. But the Judge could see that the situation was untenable; if this witness was unable to attend, the trial may have to be postponed, or even a retrial ordered. He therefore agreed that the defence witness, Gisele Dèrnier, be called immediately the court resumed that afternoon at 2pm. The judge was beginning to think that if no-one could identify the accused, then for certain the prosecution case would fail. So, he thought he might as well get the rest of the defence now and save time.

This change in order was at this stage unknown to Ann, and while her husband had arrived and tried to keep her spirits up, she was beginning to realise it would probably be down to her alone to keep Dumas behind bars and face the death penalty.

At lunch she ate very little, and by 2pm they were all back in court. Ann was about to go and sit in a room reserved for witnesses when, to her surprise, she overheard the clerk say he would be calling Gisele Dèrnier next. Having checked with Le Procureur, she went and resumed her previous seat in the gallery.

"Should you not be downstairs?" asked Richard.

"No, they are calling a defence witness. Gisele Dèrnier," said Ann.

"That's strange."

"Yes," said Ann. "The prosecutor said things had changed, but he would definitely be calling me – probably tomorrow."

\*\*

The court took some time to settle even when the judge entered. The jury members were confused, to say the least, but the judge explained about the unfortunate accident to the husband of the next witness, and asked them to be patient and listen carefully to her evidence. He said that matters were now a little back to front, but the prosecution would continue their case the next day.

Giselle was sworn in and sat in the witness box. She was a nervous as a kitten and could not stop fidgeting with her rather unruly hair.

Oliver, however, knew he had to be gentle with her to get the right answers.

"Now, Mademoiselle Dèrnier, I have some questions for you, and you must just answer my questions as best you can. There's no need to be shy."

She giggled slightly but stopped short when Oliver gave her a scowling glance. He needed to have her on a string.

"On the 16th of July, 1842, you married your husband Pierre Dèrnier, is that correct?" he asked.

"Oui, et j'avais trois demoiselles d'honneur, trois garçons de page, et ma mère est venue toute habillée comme vous n'en avez jamais vu et—."[15]

Oliver quickly stopped her. "Just answer my questions. No need to elaborate," he warned. "Now, who gave you away?"

"Mon Uncle Philippe, je pense, c'etait il y a dix-huit mois avant que j'ai eu mon Jean-Pierre." [16]

Oliver was becoming slightly exasperated but pressed on.

"Do you see your Uncle Philippe in this courtroom?"

"Oui, il est là-bas, et il m'a fait ce gros bisou."[17]

Fortunately, Jean was seated back in the gallery and Oliver purposely kept himself in position to ensure she would be looking away from the gallery, to avoid any confusion.

"Finally, Mademoiselle Dèrnier, where do you live?"

"Pourquoi, au Puy, c'est dans le sud."[18]

---

[15] Yes, and I had three bridesmaids, three pageboys, and my mother came all dressed up like you have never seen and-.

[16] My Uncle Philip, I think, it will be eighteen months before I had my Jean-Pierre

[17] Yes, he is over there, and he gave me this great big kiss.

[18] Why, at Le Puy, down south.

Oliver then quickly finished her sentence, deliberately expanding on her answer. "So, you live about 40 kilometres southwest of Saint Etienne."

"Oui, il m'a fallu toute la journée pour arriver ici, et maintenant je dois me dépêcher de rentrer chez mon mari."[19]

Oliver, looking at the judge, then said," That's all the questions I have of this witness."

Alain Lamas, the prosecutor, realised there was little hope of defeating this dotty witness. After all, a marriage certificate would show when she was married, not that he had a copy. However, he thought he would check one point.

"Mrs Dèrnier, can you advise at what time you got married?"

"Oh, je me souviens que," she said "j'enavais trois bridesmaids trois garçons de page, et il etait presque trois heures de l'apres-midi et oncle Philippe n'arrive qu'avec trois minutes a perde." She spoke with an air of triumph, as if she wanted to prove she could remember things, despite forever being told she couldn't.

The judge, seeing there were no more questions, advised her that she could step down, wished her well, and trusted her husband would make a speedy recovery.

Gisele smiled sweetly at the judge and said "merci" then was ushered out of the court to a waiting coach, which set off at great speed on the road to Le Puy.

It was at this point Oliver, thinking he was putting beyond doubt that his client was innocent, produced perhaps one would say too much information. After all, no-one was querying the date of the marriage, but Oliver was in his element and feeling elated that he had again defeated what everybody thought would be an open and shut case.

---

[19] Yes, it took me all day to get here and now I have to hurry home to my husband.

He told the judge, "Monsieur Le Président, in case of doubt about the date, here is a copy of Mrs Dèrnier's marriage certificate."

He then passed the certificate to the judge who checked the date and then passed it to the jury, who also concentrated on the date, before handing it back to the clerk of the court.

Ann, however, knew something was wrong. Sitting above the jury, she focused her eyes on the certificate as it was passed around. She could not make out many details, but thought she saw 'Chapelle Rue Emile Combes' and a stamp of the 'Prefecture de la Loire'. That must only be a few streets away up here in Saint Etienne, not down in Le Puy! The defence counsellor had duped everybody, and she even wondered if he had fooled himself by concentrating on when, rather than where, the marriage took place.

The court was then adjourned, with both the judge and jury thinking it would be a mere formality to acquit the cunning Philippe. However, Ann now knew all the pieces fitted; all she needed to do was to visit la chapelle.

"Come," she said to Jean, Richard, and Lawrence. "We must hurry. We need to see the vicar of La Chapelle en Rue Emile Combes."

The party were bemused by her request, but she almost pulled them down the stairs and, finding a coach, explained what she thought she saw. "I know he is guilty, and I can prove it. We just need to knock this alibi on the head," she told them.

It did not take long to get to the chapel, as it was only a few hundred metres from the courthouse and no more than a kilometre from the Hotel Grande.

They soon found the verger and asked to see the Marriage Register. Initially he was a little hesitant, but when the party explained that it may prove, or disprove, an alibi for a murderer, the verger went to the chapel office and brought out the books.

They turned to the 16th of July, 1842, and there was the entry for Gisele Gaillac and Pierre Dèrnier.

"Ah yes, I remember this marriage. The bride and her father were about to enter the church when this burly gentleman rushed up, gave the bride a big hug and kiss, and proceeded to push the father aside saying, 'I will give my niece away.' He was a large man, while the father was a very small man and in no position to argue, so reluctantly he let the man take the bride up the aisle. The whole episode was strange; it was as if the burly gentleman wanted everybody to know he was here."

"What time did this marriage take place?" asked Ann.

"It was due to start at three o'clock; the clock on the tower opposite was striking the hour when this 'uncle' appeared."

"So, he would just have had time to rush here from the Hotel Grande," said Richard.

"Right," said Ann, "tomorrow I will have my revenge."

At this Jean shuddered slightly. It might be revenge for Ann, but if she made her accusations in a court, it would rightly be justice.

"Come," said Lawrence, "enough excitement for one day. I think things will turn our way tomorrow. This arrogant defence counsellor had overplayed his hand. Now, it is a bright warm evening, so let me treat you all to dinner. But as I know only one café in town, *Le Café du Fleurs de Soleil,* is that acceptable to you all?"

Ann smiled. "Yes of course."

*Chapter 14*

# "Pride goeth before destruction and a haughty spirit before a fall"

**(Arrogance précède la ruine, et l'orgueil précède la chute)**

The next morning, most of the party rose early and were at breakfast a little after 7am. There was a mood of quiet defiance. Yesterday the case had all gone the defence counsellor's way, but today it was their turn.

Ann had dressed for the occasion, choosing black, but had pinned a small rose just above her right breast. Monsieur Philippe Perevade may have pieced her heart, but she was like a wounded bear that was not going to give up easily. Having breakfasted on fruit and coffee, she was ready for 'le contest'. It was the prosecution's turn today, and while she might be feeble in bodily strength, this was a 'contest' of intellect which she was determined to win and gain justice for her dear sister.

For a moment, as she looked out of the window on a rather dull morning, tears came to her eyes and a lump to her throat. It would have been her sister's 21st birthday in just another week. However, when Richard came and sat beside her, having been the only one to sleep well and thus late to the dining room, she quickly gained her composure, gritted her teeth, and said very quietly to herself, *Que la bataille commence.*

They left early for the courtroom to ensure they had seats at the front of the gallery, although this time Ann sat in the section reserved for witnesses. In fact, she was the only witness.

"Have you got everything, my dear?" asked Richard as he left her.

"Yes," said Ann, "and of course the extract from the register signed by the verger."

Even Richard did not pick up the fact that she had said 'Yes' followed by 'and', meaning she had at least two items to defeat Monsieur Philippe. He was unaware that she had the brooch and pawnbroker's ticket, which she now retrieved and put into a pocket of her dress.

At 9am sharp, Monsieur Le Président Michel Regarde entered the court, and all went quiet. The jury by now had decided their verdict. They had all questioned the evidence in their own minds and, seeing no holes, the fact that the accused was at a wedding, and no-one could tell the difference between the Perevade brothers, they just needed the foreman to do his duty and announce, "Non coupable."

The judge, however, was confounded by the evidence presented so far. He was in danger of acquitting the defendant, but felt something was not right. He knew from reading a few paragraphs on the inside of the newspapers that this man had been captured and brought back to France to face justice. But how come the gendarmerie had gone to all this trouble if this man was innocent, and it seemed his brother Monsieur Jean had not hidden from the authorities. No, there must be more to this case than simple mistaken identity.

Before going into court, the Le Procureur had advised the judge that he wanted to give his next witness a free hand to question the accused. He told Judge Regarde, "I could take instructions on each point and ask the questions, but to save the

## La Nuit à Therouanne

court's time and avoid any mistakes, will you allow Ann Carlton to, in effect, become my junior?' He then explained that Ann Carlton was the late Teresa's elder sister; Ann Montelimar before marrying.

The judge realised this was unusual but could not in practice see any procedural rule that prevented this. Indeed, not twenty years earlier it had been common practice for there to be a 'battle' in court between the accused and accuser.

Judge Regarde started proceedings slowly. He wanted to give Ann time to formulate her case, so he set the scene for her by addressing the jury.

"Yesterday in this court, you were shown a man who bears an uncanny resemblance to the man behind the bar. You also heard from a defence witness from Le Puy, a town south of here, that he was at her wedding. I believe there is much you have not learned about this terrible crime. Remember, we are dealing here with both rape and murder, and for all I know theft as well.

"You will now hear from the witness before you; her name is Ann Montelimar." The judge deliberately stated her maiden name, feeling it was about time the balance was addressed a little.

"I ask you to be patient and listen carefully to her questions and the answers the accused may give." Then with a slight wave of his hand, he told Ann. "The court is yours, Miss Montelimar."

Ann rose, but surprised the court completely by asking, "With your leave, Monsieur Le Président, I would like to read a short passage from the Bible, Jeremiah chapter 49, beginning at verse 16."

The judge was slightly surprised but was a regular churchgoer, and despite the State being non-secular, he thought a bit of spiritual guidance might be what was needed.

Ann took a deep breath and read from a small pocket Bible, speaking straight at Dumas in her mother tongue: *"La terreur que vous inspirez et l'orgueil de votre cœur, vous ont trompé, vous qui vivez dans les fentes des rochers, qui occupent les hauteurs de la colline. Bien que vous construisez votre nid comme l'aigle, à partir de là,* **je vais vous faire tomber** *dit l'Éternel."*

*("The terror you inspire, and the pride of your heart have deceived you, you who live in the clefts of the rocks, who occupy the heights of the hill. Though you build your nest as high as the eagle's, from there I will bring you down, declares the Lord.")*

She then paused for a moment, noting the mood of quiet reverence that had spread across the court. She knew she had the whole court's attention. Even the accused was sitting bemused by the whole experience and off-guard, as Ann had hoped.

Then, with a deft move like a magician, she brought the brooch out of her pocket.

"Monsieur Philippe, do you recognise this?"

Dumas was temporarily taken aback, and not thinking clearly said, "Yes, I think so. I think it is a brooch I pawned some years back."

"Indeed, you are right, for here is the pawnbroker's ticket with your name on it," Ann replied.

"Well, what of it?" said Dumas, regaining his composure. "A man's got to live."

"Yes," said Ann, "but not so others may die. This brooch was the one that my sister was wearing when you so brutally killed her."

There was a gasp from the jury.

"There must be lots of brooches like that around." said Dumas, trying to make light of the matter.

"No. There are precisely two, and they were specially made for us by a friend of our family," Ann announced. "But to be sure, you will note a small letter T for Teresa underneath."

## La Nuit à Therouanne

With that Ann, instead of showing the brooch to Dumas, passed it to the clerk, who handed it to the judge, who in turn passed it across to the jury.

"Now, Monsieur Philippe, we heard yesterday you attended the wedding of your niece. I think you use the word niece loosely, since we could not discover any relationship by marriage or blood. However, the point is you say, or rather the innocent Gisele stated, you attended this wedding at three o'clock in the afternoon and it seems ingratiated yourself on the steps of the chapel, pushing the father of the bride aside and taking his place to deliver his daughter into marriage."

"Well, it's true I even signed the register as witness. You can check, so if I was at this wedding, how could I be with your sister at the same time?" Dumas replied with a disdainful smile across his face.

Oliver Le Genaux also looked confident, convinced that Ann had tripped herself up.

Then, to everyone's surprise, she said, "Yes, you were indeed there. In fact only just got there in time; you arrived when the clock in Rue Emile Combes struck three. However, the Hotel Grande is but less than a kilometre from the chapel, and we know from the proprietor you were at the hotel at 2pm. This gave you a whole hour to rape and murder my sister, then run off to the chapel in Saint Etienne in Rue Emile Combes, not 300 metres from this court. You are a murderer, a rapist, a thief, a despicable man who has no shame. I curse you."

The court was temporarily stunned when they realised the wedding had not taken place in Le Puy, but here in Saint Etienne.

Then Ann pulled from her pocket the extract of details of the wedding, signed by the Verger of Le Chapelle Rue Emile Combes, and passed it to the judge.

"Monsieur Le Genaux, that marriage certificate, do you have it?" asked the judge.

"The clerk has it, Monsieur Le Président."

The certificate was duly produced to the embarrassment of the judge and the defence counsellor – neither of whom had noticed the place of marriage, as they had been concentrating on the date. Both papers – the certificate, and the Verger's extract – were passed to the jury who now realised that this scoundrel in front of them could not magically have been in two places at the same time.

At this point, without being given permission by Monsieur Le Président, the defence counsellor addressed the court rather than Ann.

"My client could still have been at the wedding, and someone else who looked like him at the hotel," he suggested. "Therefore, my client has no case to answer."

"Monsieur Le Genaux, I will decide if there is a case to answer," snapped the judge. "Have you finished your examination, Miss Montelimar?"

"Not quite, Monsieur Le Président."

"Very well, you may continue."

Ann took a deep breath. She had to hold her nerve and she needed the whole court's attention; she even spied the gendarme who had given evidence at the beginning of the trial. *Pillow*, she thought, and an almost wicked smile came over her face.

So, with a dramatic air worthy of France's finest actress, she said, "I will now show the court the difference between the good Monsieur Jean Perevade" – she pointed to the gallery – "and the devil seated here, Monsieur Philippe Perevade.

"The witness who will untangle this deceit and dastardly crime is my sister Teresa. It was she who wrote in her own blood the word she knew would separate the twins, because she marked one of them with her nails in her struggle. She did not write 'oreiller' as in pillow, but 'oreille' for ear – the last letter was just a smudge. If you now look closely at Monsieur Philippe, his left ear bears the scar put there by my dear sister two years ago."

Then, raising her voice, she finished her dramatic epilogue with the simple words, "J'accuse!" and pointed at the now stunned Philippe, who had forgotten the scar and was holding his ear as if to hide it from the jury.

The court, including the jury, was stunned; this petite woman had single-handedly defeated the great Oliver Le Genaux and tossed all the apparent indisputable evidence away as though it was soiled straw from a pig's pen.

Monsieur Le Président called for quiet then, leaning toward the defence counsellor, asked, "Do you wish to cross-examine this witness?"

Monsieur Oliver knew he was defeated, so there was no need to make a fool of himself any further. He shook his head. He would live another day, but regrettably, he realised his client was doomed.

Ann resumed her seat in the witness box but did not relax.

The prosecutor, Monsieur Alain Lamas, then advised the judge that his case for the prosecution was complete.

"Thank you," said the judge, who turned to Monsieur Oliver and asked, "Do you offer anything further, in defence of the accused?"

"Non, Monsieur Le Président."

The judge turned his attention to the jury. "Do you wish to retire to consider your verdict?" he asked.

The jury foreman looked around him. It was quite clear now that they had been deceived the previous day, but today everything added up. As his fellow jurors mouthed 'guilty' or drew fingers across their throats, he stood to perform his duty.

"No, Monsieur Le Président."

"What is your verdict?"

"Guilty."

With that a collective sigh and murmurings of 'too right' or 'le justice' echoed across the court.

Ann finally relaxed.

The judge called for order one last time.

"This case has been not of one, but two, or even three atrocious crimes. Merely sending you to the guillotine will seem too easy, too quick for you to show remorse for your actions, I therefore sentence you to twenty-five years in the penal colony on Devil's Island. Take this man from my sight."

And with that the judge rose. He had been despondent that he might have to let a guilty man free when he had entered the courtroom that morning, but thanks to the actions of a brave, articulate, and determined woman, justice had prevailed. Only he had noticed the tears in Ann's eyes as she had finished with "J'accuse!".

Richard, Ann, Lawrence, and Jean returned to their hotel and ordered a late lunch, as it was already 2pm. They realised that the judge had delayed his own lunch so that Ann should not lose her composure and be able to finish her evidence.

There were hugs and congratulations all round, and when the news reached the hotel, many of the guests came and personally wished Ann well for the future.

They were about to finish their lunch and rise from the table when a young lad entered the room bearing a bouquet of a dozen red roses, which he presented to 'Madame Carlton de Montelimar'.

Ann looked about the table at the three gentlemen to see who had decided to present this fitting gift, but none came forward to claim her thanks.

Then Ann read aloud the words on an attached card: "Pour le justice, avec tous mes remerciements, Monsieur Le Président."

On hearing this, the party started clapping.

"You must take this up as your career, my dear," said Richard, half joking, as he kissed her on the cheek.

"I agree," said Jean.

"Why stop there?" said Lawrence. "Why cannot La France have La Présidente?"

Ann burst into laughter. "No, no. One step at a time, or I will be accused of ideas above my station. I have enough excitement being an ambassador's wife, et peut-être une mère."

With that, Richard gave her a hug while the gentlemen offered their congratulations.

"Un toast, je pense," said Jean. "La famille."

*Le Fin*

# About the Author

**Peter Gatenby** is not yet known as an imaginative and inventive author, but more as the man who has walked everywhere. He will tell you he is the only person living or dead who has walked from his front door to the furthest points – east, west, south, and north of the British mainland, known as the Extremities in 2012/13. Then five years later to the Sharp Corners, as he calls them – that is to the furthest southwest, southeast, northeast, and northwest. The story of these epic treks will not appear in print form for some years, but will appear under the title "The Three Blue Plaques". These plaques record the foregoing achievement and currently adorn the cottage wall where he lives. In the meantime, you can still glean a lot from the websites set up to monitor these walks: www.theextremities.co.uk and www.thesharpcorners.co.uk

The first short story to be published by the author at the beginning of 2023 was *Married by Lunchtime* – a light-hearted romance with a few unusual twists and turns. This volume you have just purchased, *La Nuit a Therouanne*, is another book of fiction about the struggle to bring to justice a rapist and murderer. Both these stories are fictional, but cleverly keep the reader wondering until the last few pages how the issues raised will be resolved. However, a third book is based on real family history, starting in 1910 about the writer's maiden great-aunts who end up going to Singapore in 1925. No clever scheme to make it have a satisfying resolution, it is perhaps more a *Quantum of Solace*. The full story has been written. However, small, apparently insignificant pieces of information keep turning up.

Thus, although it might be considered more of a documentary about one family living through the early and middle parts of the 20$^{th}$ century, very often it is a living detective story. The time period is so long and fills so many pages that it is now being structured as six Episodes, under the collective banner of *The Farrells of Banchory House*. This house, the family home, stood in Old Dover Road, Blackheath, but was demolished to make way for the A102 underpass. The race is now on to try and find a picture of the house before the book goes to press.

Peter's working life of 43+ years was in Financial Services, and at the time of his retirement in 2006 he was a *Fellow of the Chartered Insurance Institute* and an *Associate of the Compliance Institute*, as well as an *Associate of the Personal Finance Society*.

Nowadays he is a member of two ramblers groups, and holds the courtesy title of Deputy Churchwarden (he has been Churchwarden on three occasions, totalling ten years' service). He is also the Chairman of The Mill Stream Villages Association (see www.TMSVA.co.uk)

When not writing or walking, he is the proud father of four children and eight grandchildren. A full house, when adding in husbands, wives, boyfriends, and girlfriends, is currently 21. Thus, utilising the skills being developed by both children and grandchildren ensures that the above volumes can be marketed, and even in due course turned into short films!

Milton Keynes UK
Ingram Content Group UK Ltd.
UKHW040612040823
426323UK00001B/75